CONVALESCENCE

A BOOK ABOUT WHAT LIFE'S ABOUT

TIMOTHY EDWARDS

Note: Parental Discretion is Advised. Recommended for readers that are 18 years and older.[2]

Published by Innovo Publishing, LLC
www.innovopublishing.com
1-888-546-2111

Publishing Books, eBooks, Audiobooks, Music, Screenplays, & Courses for the Christian & wholesome markets since 2008.

CONVALESCENCE
A Book About What Life's About

Library of Congress Control Number: 2023931947
ISBN: 978-1-61314-906-5

Cover Design & Interior Layout: Innovo Publishing, LLC

Printed in the United States of America
U.S. Printing History
First Edition: 2023

Has God called you to create a Christ-centered or wholesome book, eBook, audiobook, music album, screenplay, or online course? Visit Innovo's educational center (cpportal.com) to learn how to accomplish your calling with excellence.

Reviews of Commendation

"If you appreciate the Elvish poetry and philosophy found in J. R. R. Tolkien, then you are sure to be intrigued by the contemplative writing style of Timothy Edwards, who has the inward soul and curiosity of a modern-day Christian elf. Edwards' writing is unique in that it is not anchored in one span of time alone or buttressed in only one format of expression. What is placed upon the written page is an anthropological progression of one's wonder with the world and the God who created it from infancy to young manhood. As such, Edwards proves himself to be a neo-modern philosopher, poet, chronicler, and theologian of the issues that challenge those wanderers of the human condition in our current age where the dynamics of sexuality, faith, relationships, purpose, and meaning all intersect and often times clash. And, Edwards has a term for such a wanderer…outlier, one who struggles against the grain of accepted cultural norms and who struggles to maintain his or her integrity before the presence of God.

Warning! This book is not for the easily frightened of societal issues or for those seeking a linear writing style. Edwards' poetry style shifts effortlessly from rap to traditional. His review of issues springboard across the spectrum of lust to love. His quest is self-examination which forces the reader to examine their own heart and soul. But, be assured, all is explored with the ultimate purpose of honoring a God and Savior who is worthy.

Of Timothy Edwards and his writing, J. R. R. Tolkien might grant him the elvish title, *Istya Noleme: One of Deep Lore and Wisdom.*"

—James R. Fisher, Captain, Chaplain, USN (Ret.)

"I have known Timothy for most of his life. We first met when he was ten, and I have enjoyed watching him grow and struggle. I did not know to what extent he struggled or how deeply. After reading this book, I have a small glimpse of his inner turmoil and triumphs. Furthermore, I've even had the privilege to speak truth and give advice, which he has taken and applied to his life. I am glad I get a behind the scenes look into his life.

This is not a theology book or a book on biblical accuracy. This is a book that reveals the inner mind of a youth brave enough not only to live through life but to let people read what he is thinking. The collection of writings attempts to answer the question, *What goes on in someone's head as he struggles through life, culture, and faith?* See how a person matures through life via the mind of the person growing. Read and bear witness to his journey—but, be ready, for thoughts are private for a reason, and when stepping into another's mind, you find things that are not all kind. Reader discretion is advised."

—Jeremy Suarez, Author's Friend and Mentor

“The sights, sounds, and smells of a hospital room are offensive to some. In our health-nutrition-saturated culture, there is little tolerance for those who want to be well but for some reason aren’t, or for those who are unquestionably on the way but aren’t there yet.

You are holding a book titled *Convalescence*. To convalesce is to recover from an illness or from radical medical treatment. Indeed, Jesus came precisely to do that. He said, ‘It is not the healthy who need a doctor, but the sick’ (Luke 5:31).

My friend and brother in Christ, Timothy, has invited us into his hospital room. He is convalescing. He doesn’t pretend or play church. Diagnoses can be devastating. Some of the sights, sounds, and smells of what you read may be offensive to you. But read on! Watch the progress! Rejoice at the signs of increasing health. The Great Physician is at work!

I recommend that you read the end of the book first. I’ve never done that before! Read, ‘To Them the Closest,’ ‘Sum Up,’ along with ‘Afterword.’ These words are the doctor’s words in literary form, saying to the patient, ‘All is well. You are recovering nicely. We discovered a lot of things during the surgery, but it looks like with time, patience, and prayer, you will live out a normal life.’ For the Christian, this normal life is none other than His (God’s) very life living in and through us. I hope you will let the Great Physician work in your life. I hope you will abide by His diagnosis. I hope you will be a willing patient. And, that by the enabling of the indwelling Holy Spirit, the interceding ministry of the Lord Jesus Christ, and the endless love of God the Father, you will also live out a normal Christian life. This Christian life is explainable simply and in these terms as ‘something only God could do.’”

—Dr. Daniel D. Robinson, Pastor-Teacher-Author-Missionary

Reviews of Condemnation

“This book should have been in your hands years ago. But luckily, I’ve had the pleasure to work at Timothy since the idea of sharing his heart first entered his mind. We had some run-ins every so often, but until he proposed to release his writings, we hadn’t truly gotten close and personal. Although he pretends to not know me sometimes, we have grown right alongside each other; he’s always been such a kidder! As the publishing process is happening, we have long conversations about many things that may occur. He’s let me help him with some of his ideas like the rejection that’s sure to come, the misunderstandings people will have that he can’t always explain clearly, and especially the adversity: the spiritual and relational strains that are guaranteed when trying to be obedient to our “callings.” But try as I might to keep him from forcing this book on the public, he seems to be empowered from something I don’t understand, to do what I can’t talk him out

Shalom!
Here is a page for you.
It's your dedication page. Make it exactly that.
Your Book. Sign your name, spit on it, draw something sick,
but
M A K E I T Y O U R S. This isn't anyone else's.
Neither is anything else. If you don't like something
remove it, mar it, extirpate it.
Auf Wiedersehen.

INTRODUCTORY FORMALITIES

The world is in ruins…but I wrote a book! Truthfully, there have been so many factors in my writing and almost not writing this. Living in the top percentile of every existing strata in the world (social, cultural, economic, etc.) made me very hesitant to give my little addition. Ultimately, however, it came down to obedience. God, beyond my understanding, has given me a gift that I've loved to use and develop. For a while, I was content with it remaining just a skill I had and didn't need to do anything I didn't want to with. But, as He used it to bring me closer to Him and the others around me, He also granted me the desire to share it with others. I can't think of anything better to do than show how God has worked in my life and document it in an art form that I can't stop loving.

I am so thankful to get to be thankful for my parents. They have trained up their children in the way they should go, and any wrong-doing of mine is in no way a reflection of their parenting. They have made the hard calls their whole lives, and I will be set if I heed their wisdom even slightly. Thank you guys for protecting me, being patient with me, and giving me space to find and do what I love.

My sister. Now there's a book that needs to be written! You've been my counterpart and fellow culprit for my entire existence. I pity with my utmost those who haven't gotten to grow close with their siblings because it's been a hilarious and painful and well-worth-it ride. Thanks for not sending me back!

Grandma Dawn, I do not use the word *cherish* anywhere else in this book. That is the only way I can describe how I feel about our times we share. You're a beautiful plethora of laughs and advice and heartfelt-ness, and I hope I get to be a lot like you. Thank you for realistically supporting me and graciously telling me how it is, Sicilian style!

Thank you to my four completely awesome uncles who give me all sorts of advice and help me with my stupidity and make me laugh to painful points. You guys have been huge role models for me on what not to do (ha!) and especially on what to do in my uncle-ing career. Michael, Aunt Bobbie, Gabby,

Jarred, Brandon, Jordan, Jacob, Jonas, Juniper: you have all been patient and loving and generous and helped me stay wise and young!

To Joshua, Kaylen, Landon, Andrew, and Devin. You guys are my few friends who have been by me through life's craziness and writing craziness and my craziness. Thank you for being yourselves and letting me be myself. It's been super cool to have God bring the right people in and out of my life in His timing, and you guys have helped me realize I'm not the hero at the end of the story. He is. And I believe we'll all be able to simply be thankful when it all comes to a close.

To everyone who has known my family and me and helped support us: thank you so much for being faithful and serving with us. I could write multiple books on how you have changed my life and outlook, and this would not be in your hands without your influences.

To everybody who has helped me on the book, I cannot thank you enough! Dr. Dahmer, I am beyond grateful that God crossed our paths for one, but also that you would step out in faith to help me publish this. It is a serious risk any way you look at it, and I'm rendered speechless that you would use your gifts and business to assist me in my writing endeavors. Mrs. Rachael, I am so deeply thankful for your inputs and advice, and I apologize for giving you such a task as this to review! You've been ever patient, and I'm far more than appreciative for your help. For all the others at Innovo who have been working on this project without me even realizing it, I thank you from the very core of my being!

To those who have endorsed this book, you have been the primary motivators to steer me back to finishing this book to completion. Chaplain and Mrs. Fisher, thank you both for showing me God has given me one of His talents. Mr. Suarez, you've been an immobile beacon reflecting Christ's light for me, and I thank you for always keeping me in check. Preacher Dan, you have had a huge influence on 2 generations of this family, and you have been incredibly supportive of my writing process. Thank you for gently pointing me in correct directions and teaching the Word obediently.

FOREWORD

Timothy Edwards is a very special young man. It has been an honor and a privilege to share his life. He is loving, caring, honest, kind to a fault. He is extremely devoted to God and his family. I am very proud of his accomplishments.

He has a unique way of doing things. From the time he was a little guy, he spoke his own language. For instance, when he said "deet deet," we knew he was getting ready to jump off of something. His book is like he is, interesting, insightful, informative, funny.

It has been a delight to have spent time watching him grow up and to be his Grandma Dawn.

—Dawn Greene

Is it Poetry? If
The words aren't merged in timelessly
Our feelings aren't stirred up violently
Its gist isn't imaged rhymelessly
If it's grimy, slightly slimy: Like mud in the sun while drying
Is it strong as a diamond I-beam?
Twisted as conch shell ivories?
Maybe savory as a tasty treat from a bakery to a sailor be braving the Aegean Sea
Is it years to discern, decades to learn?
All that we need, or shall it be burned?
Rare as alabaster, yet inquizzically childish
Requiring two lives to master, evident in the second's eyes' eclipse
From blessing beyond all measure, Or madness past just imbalance
To be polished and relished as treasure, Or the heartwork of talentless regalants
Or maybe, just for disputation's sake does it exist
So as to refute those who refuse beauty within their midst
Can the kids comprehend it? Or must "adults" first give their examinings?
What will we inherit from our descendants? To give's the quintessence of parenting
We will recite it? We can live by it? We leave our angles beside it?
Countless, Copious queries
May culminate
Yet
Is it
Still Poetry
If
We
Find
It
?

1/29/20 2/18/20

2/4/20

Poetry is Dead – We blew open her head

To figure out the pulp and neurons, but we can't make sense of it – Go to work and serve Mexican – Go back to our houses which were built by them – Give it funky names, but we still end up paying rent – Going to bed content with our negligence – Ever catch yourself preening your wounds? To keep the people you don't need around and amused – Tell someone that you've never met "This emotional mess is a ruse" – Everyone's making such a fuss – Not even seeing, it's calamitous – But every one of us would just shut up if we knew we're just the earth's purulence – Positivism's what we oughta doubt – Lest we skip and sing our way out to the slaughterhouse – Cause all from progress that we found is that it makes more ways for opting out –

Listen to the prophets of gloom and doom
Cause I believe in the Thief and think He's coming soon
But if they relay there's no hope for you
Then my friend Load, AiM, AND
fume
Lol
We're an abscess on reality
Reared in the absence of causality =
Effectless flotsam and some acrid meat
As each other's broody neighbors sadly dragging dreams

The blessed irreverent will always feel at home – But for the restless penitent their even keel's to roam – So I ask you Tabithas, what did you learn on your own? – Talk all night, I'm still convinced you're just another clone – If that's uncomfortable stick to your one-night stands – Just don't go off the Banzai cliff, none who are true wish for you in Saipan – Block inside, outside, low, high, and knife-hand – Royalty is overruled when only low-lives can

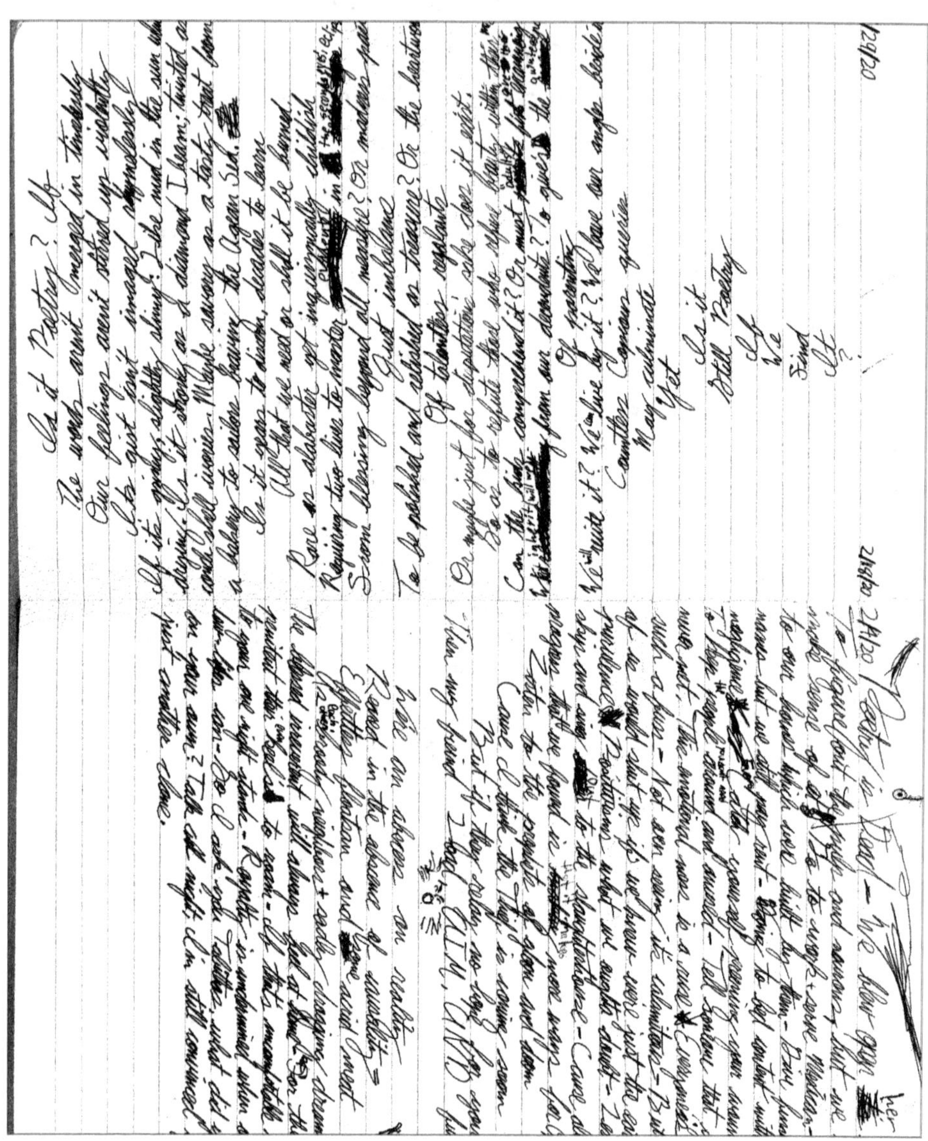

Figure 1. Is it poetry if

12/24/16

Crows swarm the dead apple trees
Angels in black swim the dull, stone-faced sea
We trek the dust-ridden, rocky lane
To tread amongst the granite statues of pain
Weathered and wind-worn, polar and polished
Resolute she takes her stance with the fat and the impoverished
Perpendict with all the others, I take the full sight round
As my father's phrase within me prays
"She is not in the ground"

1/13 – 17/17

My, how the times have shifted
As the shelves which prowl under the sea.
Most have tossed tools which had sifted
To expose all new darkness beneath

My, how this land's kept distracted
From the beauty that they could achieve.
So enthralled with what's at arms' distance,
Tread upon what has been bequeathed.

My, but the things which are steadfast
Need new edges to sharpen their point.
The vitals can't be forced to relax
Those been imparted cannot always avoid.

11/5/16

Cease not laughing my younger brother
Never lose your joviality.
Because older, we think we're smarter
But what if you are wiser than we?

13th of the 4th month in the year of our Lord 2021
Sig-Net-Nature

I believe I'm blessed, but will I when things get wild?
I know that I know God, but do I need Him like a child?
He loved me more than I could ever love my sin.
He never even flinches when I try to make Him wince.
How could I not ache and strain when all that must change
Is Within?
Just symptoms, symptoms, symptoms, symptoms, symptoms, Fruit
Of sickness, sickness, sickness, sickness, sickness, Root
With sundry weapons for wielding, possessions for shielding
My only points for referencing
Are my Natural Tendencies
All I've been in is Human Nature
I only know what's natural to Sin Nature
But what if I were sealed with a SigNature?
And not a knock off, rip off caricature

But it's a bit irregular to transfigure, similar in station to transformation. Both originating from a language overseas, known in Greek vernacularly as metamorphose = it's more than to transpose, it's entire alteration, it's character change, but not of itself it's by the giving of Grace. Dissimilar infrastructure, disparate DNA. Though the gas tank and the glass make their living betwixt empty and full, by/ through/ with His bounteous profuseness we may live devoid of null!

Mortal body
How you fail me!
Bone and flesh
I must endure.
Disattach my soul and body
For my mind was made for more
9\/17\/16

2/16/17 - 3/30/17
Celestia

死
亡
临
近

It began as such; divine supreme. A place incomprehensible by this generation. A world without race or government or provinces. The land swept clean yet lacking soiled history. There, a man was seen as truly equal to his neighbor. Impossible may be the first word to define such a utopian region. But like every earthly country, it is not the landscape which comprises the area, it is without fail, the residents of that area. The hard-working fathers who teach their sons how to maintain love and security and kindness conjointly. Of course, the mothers who lead as ladies, and who peaceably steer the miniscule faults of her offspring. And as one they make a home. As one they make a society. Do not forget the daughters who must feel love and purpose at their back. Or the sons that need acceptance and respect from those around them. They learnt how to learn and how to impart learning and teachable spirits to others. People's traits and oddities were not looked down upon. Questions were welcome, and statements had grace. Knowledge and wisdom walked hand in hand with simplicity and clarity. Everyone had something to offer, and smiles were as commonplace as thanks given.

Here, the scenery seems contrary to anything the modern man knows. The grass grows softer than silk, but it is not permitted to rise higher than the ankle by the sun. Underlying soil here is as if it were pre-decomposed and left heavenly nutrients below. Trees elongate, ascend, latch on the sky. The mountains rake the clouds.

Forest floors have no weeds. The wavelike plains break only with pure water streams. The shore greets immense oceans, and the crystalline depths gape untouched. The view from the beach towards land directly compares to the sight from the mountaintop towards sea. No blemish exists in the landscape. Skies envelope the earth more than panoramic photographs could capture. Night brings alive the heavenly hosts. Then, the galaxies model their artwork. Not one can overlook the ethereal show, they cannot but be convicted of their true minuteness.

This world is like nothing we can fathom. No machines or modern technology, for there is no need of them. It is too dry to sweat, but too humid for unwarranted fire. The ground supplies necessities and the surrounding waters are clear of harm. Insects which would now demolish wooden structures are unheard of. Rot and decay are no worry, and the sun does not make brittle the constructions. Pollution is but an imaginable nightmare. The storms come quickly and achieve their purpose. The rains replenish the earthen floor, yet do not sweep away sediment in their egression. Winds pick up airborne imperfections, but softly caress a playful youth. Thunder inspires the tempo of instruments, and lightning produces power in the bodies of its onlookers. Snow is perceived as the epitome of the atmosphere's true view of man; no two alike but amount to nothing if kept separated.

This world's denizens will seem to us to act out a lifestyle of the past. Their residences have grass as their floor and the windows need no glass to keep away the outdoors. The amount of land owned by a person or family is proportionate to how many people live there. People live off their plots while still being free to hunt beasts of the forests and capture marine creatures and snare the fowl above. The surrounding oceans are not salty and are magnificent to drink. People are at liberty to explore their homeland for all of its beauty and unknown secrets. Natives of this territory protect and do not harm the landscape, for they know they were only entrusted with one homeland. But it is realized that the ground and water and sky are incomparable to a single human life. Thus, they nurture and partake of the nature around them, but would never propose to worship it.

This world is, quite literally, unintelligible to humanity at its present juncture. When life begins in -------- , everything is perceived to a higher degree by a new boy or girl. They will never encounter sickness during their lifetime. Learning anew will be simplified inside their minds. Color approaches young eyes with a wider prism than we can engender. Labor is not questionable for all caretake their own bloodline and assist the well-being of the collection. Senses are enhanced, for there is nothing to prohibit them from being ultra-instinctive. Their physical ability is enhanced because they don't eat or drink anything to restrict themselves. As they mature, none of them are outcasts, and every human is a component of the group. People are accepted not in spite of, but because of their unique characteristics. Young adults are free to work, study, play, and contemplate for themselves; their elders realize that they must make their path themselves but would never venture to not love them enough to correct. At last, boys truly treat young women with the respect they deserve and have learned to give, and girls are finally able to have faith in the trustworthiness of young men.

One may consider the theory that those outside of this world and its hardships could not fully appreciate depth of life and understand true beauty. But, whenever we on this planet think of profound ideas and dream of superior imaginings, do we not attempt to rid our minds of and pursue beyond the darkness of our world? We propose that if nothing bad or distracting were in our way, we could accomplish so much more for ourselves and others. This is everyday life for the people of -------- . They work enough to live out healthy lives, provide responsibility and stability to their kind, and then proceed to devote themselves wholeheartedly to search their minds of profundity. They sleep only as much as is necessary, and then plot the courses of the sun's cousins. We picture this realm as utterly unrealistic, but is it not what every person actually desires? Is this world not corroborative of our innate longings? Is it not what we could ever hope for? Picture the calmness in one blink of a child there. Imagine the untroubled sense as you exit your hand-built home. Envisage the love felt for personal and public history with hope and excitement for the peaceable times that are sure to arrive.

People on Earth could never transition from here to there while having lived a conscious life here. Our past life would bar the perfection of this region. If you were born, however, in this wonderful land, you could enjoy and behold all that it has to be held. You could study the land, you could roam the vast ocean, you would have uninhibition and clearness to think in ways unique and special. You could be thought of as whatever you want, and people would accept you for that. You could find love. No distractions could hinder you from that which you desire. You would finally have all that you ever wanted. Happiness could never leave you again.

There is though, one flaw in the essence of this university of existence. In spite of otherworldly health in food and drink and utter lack of contaminant in the air, the "human" bodies residing there still deteriorate and ultimately perish. Even though their age of death varies, they meet the same ending fate as we on Earth. No matter how hard they tried and avoided death, it always enslaved them. Even the most brilliant mind in another reality meets death at his appropriate time.

What if we could truly obtain everything we ever wanted?
Maybe some of us could create a world better than --------- . Maybe we could have all riches known to man, or we could own every inch of land on this planet or another. Maybe we could just finally be happy or finally be everything we dream of being. We could now feel heard and accepted, loved, and respected in any way you choose. Anything, Anyway, Anytime, Anywhere, with Anybody. Do as you desire.

One thing will never stop haunting your perfect life. You will still Die. Your world closes with your eyes. Your time ceases when your blood takes its last circuit. Evading, it is the impossible. Your soul abandoning your body is one of the few assured promises.

In light of its limit then, everything being "perfect" pales. Even if everyone got everything they wanted, it amounts to nothing if it ends. Being completely satisfied in this life means nothing if it ends.

This is why in a ghastly world we can always have hope for a better life after death. But, even in a "perfect" realm, we must always see that if it ends, there is always something more.

欢
迎
死
亡

Figure 2. Tree of my life

9/18/17 – 9/27/17

Observing Anew

Oh! Those old sights
Soon looked upon, till then blocked by subconscious.
Thus overlooked, half the world wisps away.
A fate worse than death, whilst time on the earth,
Draws closed the curtains, keeps full life at bay.

For longer, fixate
Remember world's past and imagine forthcomings.
See, hear, and taste, smell and touch all anew.
Rejuvenation of mind brings beauty of life.
This verity brings all that is true.

11/15/17 – 11/16/17

My Curse

So much I love you – already know
And I'll use our entire lives to show
Just to what extent my love will go
Oh, but you do, don't you – already know
Though here's something I know that you don't
My curse is how I labeled it, rated it
Still hate and hated it, questioned and debated
It's existence and finished, settled upon
The idea of it being parallel with the total
And final void of your relatability to my
Case known as You.
Cause let's face it, I'm stupid – Yeah, you're
So out of my league – You should have served
Me your justice, but you dished grace and mercy
Now we're past that, beyond that
Still trying to just ignore that I failed you – my favorite

And I just might every day on, though somehow
You choose my side azures to lean on
I just won't ever understand it and that's the
First of my curse,
yet the rest is consisted of
The same thing in reverse.

9/26/18

DeFLEXioN

Ft.

t = d/s Kaylen Williams Date: Unknown

Seismic. Earthquakes are the result of compounding tension. See there is growth in patience, boundless energy in the silent. Solitude is the ultimate benefactor of productivity. Staying out of sight

...

Out of mind if you will and allowing the surface to speak for itself. Time is a commodity, not a luxury. It can be sought and sold on even the poorest known markets. Our budgets are the same, limited, yet the optimal bundle is fluid in everyone. What I do with mine, and you with yours simply cannot Connəct. Isn't it strange then that the ground underneath your feet is shifting? Rumble young man, Rumble...

Enter T- Kinda squirrely but not as curly as Shirley Temple. No badge or central appendage up as my credential. Raising Cain, though no Adam, so no raising Abel. A bit unstable but still saving the mental data, enslaving the false sheep, and shaving 'em in the stable, down to the naked skin; all these canines who slay rhymes but never come to an end... they've got no point, kinda like a wall-point pen. A band of bandits handing out their contraband. I gotta hand it to 'em, their brand of canned goods is ($*)#*$, good. But if I'm being candid, I can't stand it, because all we really get to savor will always be a bland flavor – and I know that people hunger for a tray full – of

hope, so I opened a buffet labeled "All y'all come and get it by the plate-full!" It's wasteful, all the inedible gibberish filling up the table – Better yet, it's disgraceful – this hullaballoo, jumbling mumbled babble will only get oohs and aahs – and really it ain't that far – and really it's not that hard – to thread lyrical yarn – and knit over-worded scarves – Where the difficulty starts – is hoisting what's on your heart – and putting it on display in the most memorable way so that it won't come off easy like a sleezy lady's panties – that takes no careful planning – It's slim picking the difference between the screwed hooch and abused pooch – it's lose-lose news but hey, it's up to you to choose – My sincere apologies for acting as a douche – I'm just attempting to prove how smooth one can fuse their thoughts and views, and spew them into the minds of our youth: no matter how skewed – It's unsettling but it's the upsetting truth – and unexpectedly, some fools are still unsuspecting – but to be honest, it's probable and probably plausible, the probability of me borrowing all the words which my alphabet can afford – and using them all for one purpose and one accord – it still couldn't be a feasible theory to ever make people see clearly – hear ye, how I've been sheltered – my face swelters telling how I was homeschooled – socially uncool? I wrote the book – you're reading it, it's my tribute and revolt – my sister and I might be uncultured, but minorities aren't the cult – fix your occipitals – get critical, like when I visited the Citadel – untypical, these clauses being so deep they're abysmal – every dirigible syllable indicative and inimical – unlimitable but inhibited from being inimitable – illegible yet so indelible riveted with illiterate and unequivocal – let's get minimal, quit all the amenities, unnecessities, living in an anemone, sipping lemon and tea, never quit swimming, in incessancy, synonyms for dips in the inseminate sea – my head's in the clouds up above Bespin you see?
Not yet... the con caved in and got it complex – you don't like

this, don't worry, yours is on next – I'm just stepping outward, the coward's convex! See this that deflect, reflex, devoid of defects – people are content thinking that all that they need's sex – not a knight of Ren, but I'm pretty even – everybody's putting out, I go inward in my evenings – everyone around me getting stoned like Stephen – didn't wrong them, but I'm trying to repent – how could we all be American rejects? – so let's just try to meet ends in a sequence – not to relent but to cement we are needed children of the King and He's the Meaning. He's the Reason and between their teeth they're seething, but He supplied them with the air that they're breathing – and no matter how well they're
seasoned, it'll be them, not Him, who is leaving

11 / 3 \ 17

There is one sufficient reason, I believe, to treat with more respect than is deserved, those who unjustly condemn us and they who we define as lowlier or more stupid than ourselves. We do just that, on all sides of thought; we degrade and dismiss others' ideas which we do not immediately accept. Not only do we ignore their thoughts, but we deem them as persons below ourselves. Woe upon us who practice these things! For our respect towards others should be immovable. Let not one of us presume to comprehend what has made a human so. All of our thoughts, feelings, and actions at someone with which we disagree would be deeply and truly altered if we realize we would be Just Like Them. Had we been born by their parents and they to theirs, into their families, among their friends, taught by their mentors, loved the same people, enjoyed the same entertainment, ate the same food and downed the same drink, been hurt the same way, been inspired equally, hoped the same hopes, dreamt identical dreams, worn the same styles, read the same words, laughed with parallel laughs, cried the same tears, heard the same sounds, sniffed the same smells, seen the same sights, touched the same things. Had we felt what they've felt, then we'd think what they've thought. And if we think the same things, we would act the same ways. No matter how wrong we all one day might be...

Unbiasedly,
T. R. Edwards

11/19/17
"Amidst many deciding factors, reading will make one a Real Man" – Dawn Greene

"We should have an Intercultural National Convention every Sunday morning" – Ted Edwards

12/6/17

The Mattress- Burial Conundrum

That is true; there does seem to be a certain correlation between the two. In a direct comparison to those objects which people used to recline on, the humans of today are certainly pampered relating to that on which they now sleep. And still more so when held next to the vast majority of society in the world today, who sleep upon anything to make themselves more comfortable. Not only do the more blessed people of today sleep upon luxurious sofas, but they actually possess the ability to choose among thousands of options of mattresses on which they decide to set their slumber. Here they vary upon width, vary upon breadth, vary upon length, vary upon comfort. Selections galore exist to determine thickness, density, texture, and even factors to associate themselves personally to these objects. The recliners then have the capability of covering these mattresses with beautifully colored coverings. Then they adorn them with plush pillows as if they were not so comfortable by themselves. Then these are placed within all sorts of designed frames and with elaborate headpieces all for the purpose of being more appealing to the viewers. They are then placed in the center of rooms and more pieces of furniture are positioned with the bed in mind, and the color scheme is chosen in relation to the comforter's. People will decide their houses upon the size and condition of these "bedrooms." But indeed, there is an odd connection between the increased number of mattresses produced and sold and the decrease of the deceased being buried in the average conventional manner. But as always, readers, enjoy your slumber supremely.

1/13/18
My writings will serve a terrific purpose: kindling, perhaps, or possibly a prop for greater things.

It is best to teach how to learn.

To see the meaninglessness and yet the collateral purpose of one's life is always single-handedly powerful enough to drive me to the feet of He who determines worth.

?/?/?
Do you know how many people had to fall in love for me to find you?

2/20/18 – 2/23/18

Rough Draft

Bluer then blue, yes: the purest azul. Every blue shade remade is a replica of perfection in you. Too dark for the sky from here and too light for the seas from there. They are the horizon locked between ocean and air. It looks like time from the past and to the future collided in spheres of the ultimate color, brilliantly in a paused supernova encircling the sincere black hole. Perhaps heaven's banner palette was hung replicating the gates to your mind? The essence of color:
to be only beheld by the spiritual realm. They're startling, harboring sights of the universe we may never capture:
collapsar stellar ransacked galaxies graffitied so celestially,
Elysian noval nebulous panoramas can't contain, kaleidoscopic

andromedae, searing ballistic meteors singeing the space-time equilibrium, electrical phenomena shearing gaseous skyscapes, spanning planetary and lunar systems, solar cycles sinking soundly, vaulting proudly, miraculum so unfathomable all found in lofty orbs, surrounding the dark door to your spirit's soul so spectacularly. Yes, please, pardon me, the violence around your iris overwhelms and condemns my unworthiness to observe them. The holiness in your retinas illuminates me as inadequate, they radiate the beta rays, alpha + gamma radiation waves. They suffocate while resonating, at high rated frequencies they burn, rend, render, and scathe me, conflagrate me, and I ache under the display of your gazing: I'm sorry.

Cause almost in an instant, instantly, immediately succeeding my being having been frayed, there's an instance where your eyes image and blanket my pitiful remains. While I'm mesmerized, itemizing, + idolizing those Geminis, the twins so tenderly caress me in the most blest efference deeming me to rise from my kneeling reverence. They welcome me as if I've deserved their privilege, pushing me to better myself for betterment's sake. I scant can understand how you don't glance at me askance, but I can't share their ideas, can't shake the I + Me = unworthy, ashamed mindset. Thus, I look elsewhere instead. But it's not about who I am, it's about how far your love accepts. It all occurs in a segment of a second, and every time our eyes meet it happens again.

3/29/18

Cordial condemnation is the most popular form of judgement in the church.

3/2/18

I suppose I was born with a silver spoon inside my mouth. Though my dad was born with a gun in his, I'm glad he decided to take it out.

2/28/18

Slumber Problem

I mean, yeah, sure, that's just a metaphor- If it lets you sleep easier under those cozy covers of yours- Sleeping well is a skill I've just recently taken up- I've had slumber problems all the way since day one- I remember listening to lullabies when I was 3- I knew there were 17 tracks on the CD- I tried to coerce myself to sleep, keeping my eyes squeezed- When that album would quit rotating, I would begin to cry- I realize now I was creating my own lullaby

Why

Pain, and in living; Sorrow
Never hopes to see the
Morrow-
Gratefully accepting the unknowns
There are to die
Cannot comprehend, what it
Means to mean the end
Have then lost
Their reason
Why

Onward, ever-sighting
Forward constantly
Though fighting
Brush past temporal troubles
Pondering, not, to shrink or shy
Bright; hopes, looks upon the future
Waits to see what fate could procure
Never lost
Their reason
Why

Why, unlike others, is pressing on
It's past the depth and feelings; beyond
The brain and heart- the soul and mind
Why is not hostage to space and time
If you have breath, then Why is inside it
Although it dwells in us, I hope that
You find it

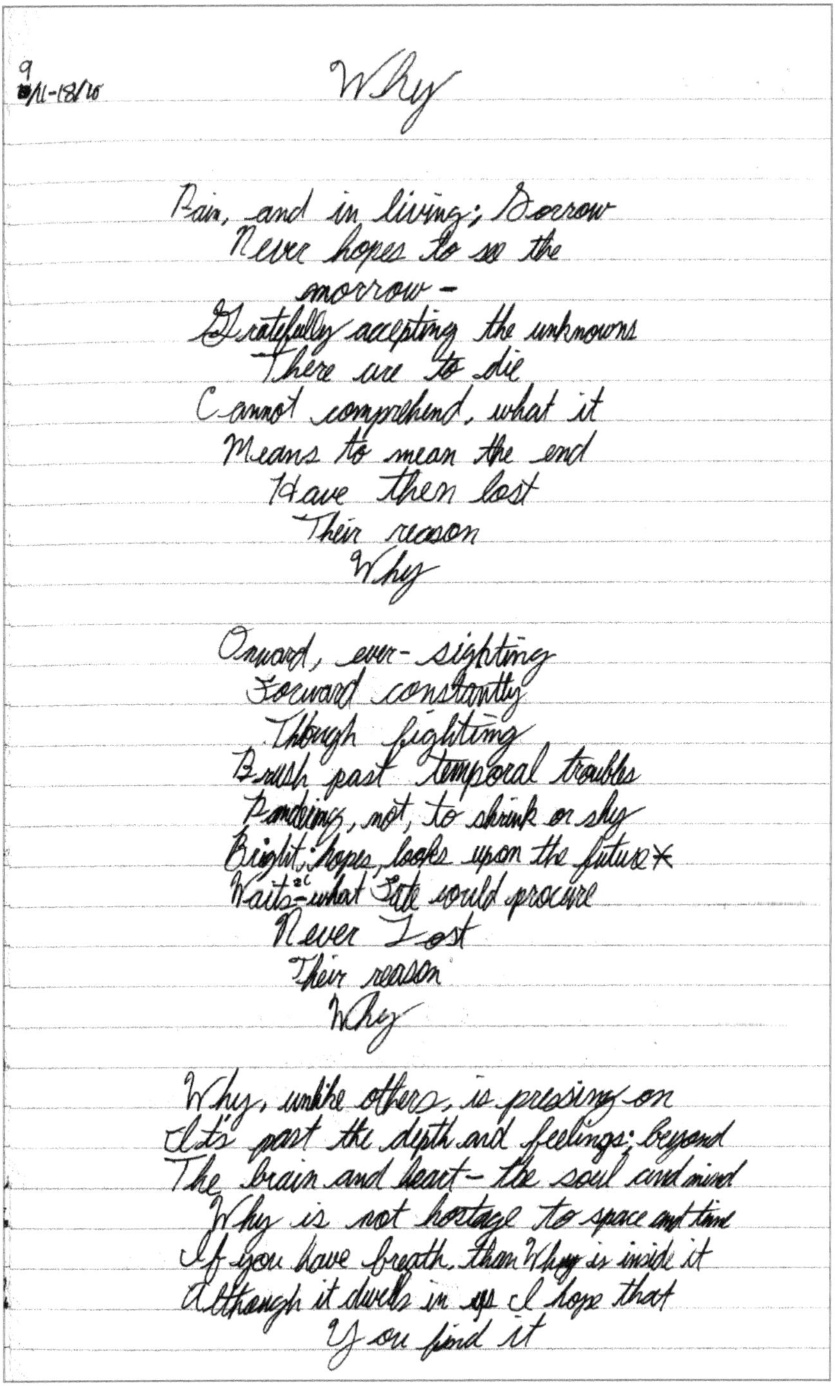

9/11-18/10

Why

Pain, and in living; Sorrow
Never hopes to see the
morrow -
Gratefully accepting the unknowns
There are to die
Cannot comprehend, what it
Means to mean the end
Have then lost
Their reason
Why

Onward, ever-sighting
Forward constantly
Though fighting
Brush past temporal troubles
Pondering, not, to shrink or shy
Bright hopes, looks upon the future*
Waits-what fate would procure
Never Lost
Their reason
Why

Why, unlike others, is pressing on
It's past the depth and feelings; beyond
The brain and heart - the soul and mind
Why is not hostage to space and time
If you have breath, then Why is inside it
Although it dwells in us I hope that
You find it

Figure 3. Why

2/22/18 – 2/23/18

There are a lot of you trapped and I've got the key- I'll help you get out and then you'll see- There's nothing this world has worth purchasing- that's the whole point of this living thing- once we see life ends, then suddenly we can start living free- you can try therapy- you can buy industries- literally you can try anything- and still miss out on everything- I'll hear your complaining- I hear what you're saying- I'll tell you the same thing- That the fact isn't changing- He is consistently, simply waiting.

"He doesn't know of the dark," why? Because I chose an abode that sits in the light?- No, I just picked out the life which was farthest from the one I was wallowing in, alright- And I am just now, starting to get out- from under the rock that was holding me down – so now I am running away- but I'll revisit it just for your sake- just don't get angry when I will not stay, ok- It had become unbearable for me to remain- in that place where devils reside- it's no secret, they don't have to run and hide- sure, you wanna know why?- For I stood on my porch and said y'all come inside!

8/16/19

My! But those eyes - Pinched in the horizon
Where the sea's ceiling - And the ground of the sky
Together, that sliver of where they collide
Engender that pigment = my one true
Goodbye

3/3/18

Suffocating, strangulating, complete lack of capacity for inhaling; only swallowing water; burning in my trachea and overwhelming my nasal cavities; trickling down the slopes of my lungs flanking my heart speeding its tempo superseding

and eradicating my oxygen supply pulsing my extremities slowly lulling me to sleep sinking with the liquid filling me to equalize with my surrounding eyes fading ey s f ding y s a i g
e f n e d s

Figure 4. Terms for my surrender

Why do I keep coming to God with terms for my surrender?

5/9/18 –

My Credentials

I must start out by saying; it's a miracle
I made it
My parents made their ways in Dante's
9th and final spiral of Sheol
But I think that's theirs to tell
Early life wasn't bad
But sleep became an issue
So many wasted hours
I spent crying in the night
Spurned on a darkness in me
Caverns called solemnity are where I'd spend my time
Though the worst part about it
Was I wasn't even 9
Years it went on = dark and then light,
I could never decide in which one to reside
When my only sibling left to pursue
Her higher education,
I felt like I was abandoned
So I made my life martial arts
And developed my mind and body
I started to develop and love myself
Yet hated me simultaneously
Then I got Burnt
So like a Ronin I loned it
And was brought lower than ever
Before
Then I found God
Or I guess He found me
I was finally free

Or so I thought
A few months of Joy
In which I indulged
Then death kidnapped my Mamaw
My false bridge of hope
Cracked and collapsed underneath
Sadness welcomed me back
My dad was torn down and
His brothers weakened
Purpose hid from me
A couple of months did I fall
I had a few questions
And then those questions were answered.
Turned out I was heading
Towards a head-on with cancer
Still fresh of when we got the call
It was a false alarm
I'd just injured myself pursuing my
Dreams too hard
The anguish
Mental turmoil and a sense of hopelessness
Held me up and buried me
My life seemed so devalued
It clouded me from truth
Then my purge began
Dropping people like hot potatoes
Maturity came down on me
Rearranging like a tornado
I always felt like an outsider
Real life came and confirmed
These people had no capacity
To comprehend what I'd learned =

Our next breath ain't guaranteed
So, I backed out of the crowd
And started to make my way
Left some of me behind, but I'm
Glad of how it turned out
For a while but then summer came around
Like an idiot I embraced emotion
Trying to feel my way through life
Like antennae floating in the ocean
I was getting nowhere
But nearing darker avenues
One relationship blossomed while another seemed to
Be falling apart
Which took me to Depression Street and
Anxiety Boulevard
I invested my attention in an unworthy cause
All that "friendship" left me with was
The feeling of being robbed
Then my sister was wedded, but I had a bad feeling
I still hope that intuition never ends up being for good reason
Not even a month
And my grandma was struck
It's as if she couldn't truly
Laugh for a time after that
After a summer of action
We hoped the shuffling would end
But my mother was dealt cancer
And she was relieved of her rank
We were always drifting apart
But I had no idea what to say
The worst night's sleep of my life was on
Her procedure day

Awake, lying and crying with no choice but to pray
Once in a lifetime chance came and I stole it
Finally pushing my body, taking all they were doling
My mind began to ride along and
Then my soul unfolded
Just when I was satisfied in my position
Along came a girl who gifted me with an illness
She thieved my heart so calmly though
We knew she'd have to go
Weeping in the pitch-black cul-de-sac
I hated what I couldn't know
One friend appeared to be throwing away his marbles
Another seemed to not wish to be a part of my world
The third stooge stood by me all of the way through
Not to replace blame
But a lonely summer left me alone
A holy soul-sized hole was deftly exposed
So, I let temptation be my company
Eventually my faults caught up with me
I confronted and opened up to all the people
Who weren't supposed to see
Coming clean to all the folks
Whose perception meant the most to me
Heaven tattled having to battle the things
That had been controlling me
My parents and therapist tried to counsel me
But inbred hatred and derangement were the ones who consoled me
Everyone said draw close to God, but I was more than happy ignoring
The very people who wanted the best for me
Time came around, not to heal my wounds

But I guess just to give me some distance and breathing room
All the while, Trevor was growing up in the womb
December 5th, that was when chaos ensued
I can clearly recall Andy's face when he gave us the news
Hands and knees on the hospital floor
As they took his son's body- was the strongest man I knew
No idea how to help, didn't have even a clue
Keeping the places clean was the best we could do
Grandpa's call topped it off and all it accomplished was to delude
Just a couple days later in the embrace of my boo
Got back, no time to relax as we started to move
My friend beat us to it, we gave respect as was due
Dad's crash, almost was his last would have been far too soon
A few months spent decaying; I hate to say of no use
Recently anxiety's been trying to
Decide which future I'll pursue
Fear, his twin brother's been bullying me into
Having something to prove
Got a wrestle, stressful job and been rocking at new school
Been being ok but sweating what's truly true
Now it's been a few minutes with everything going smooth
I can't stand how I take for granted the parts of me that accrue
Ad Infinitum the selections I can pen on the last TWO
My "favorite forever twice over" but He said we must say adieu
Issues out the wazoo but no room cause I'm losing count
But must mention the second semester
When mom read the letter aloud
Cancer has rung the bell, she's onto the second round
Can she please rest for just a second?
Her head's still a wreck from the clout
Honestly, me and dad were worried she wouldn't want to win this bout

But she purchased and returned it and we couldn't be more proud
She disobeyed her doctors; we say she took the scenic route
While we awaited results, dad had a breach in his hull
A hole had blown open his colon and I spent almost a week alone
Fever, virus, pneumonia just so it runs in the whole
New people and new endeavors, I've been pleasured to play a role
I certainly pray that they may thrive in Nashville
He is giving me freedom to pick the best direction to cull
7/16/20 – Almost a year since my last input, I find that pitiful
That's cause God has let us breathe + our blessings have been plentiful
Though we haven't trusted it,
Like an abused dog when a kid tries loving it
Now it's like I'm on the suffix and because of it I've hunkered
in their bunker where the truth is I'm usurped and disruptive
But everybody's 2020's been so cruddy
They've been making it out like they're bunked with cousin Dudley
I think it's funny cause once everyone is struggling
My few friends and folks have just gotten the good times bumping
School's in the past; was just for laughs
Cause everything I need to know follows no career path
My best friend's baby has emerged, my heart's welled up and glad
I have my demo/reno project: finally a risk to which I said yeah
I cleared the chamber
I love the muzzle free, but there might be one in the mag
Over and over I ask the back of my forehead:
"<u>How do I want to want God?</u>"
When I always want what I don't have?
I tried so hard to be Christ's lawyer, yet His Witness is what He asked
He proffers me with freedom from my sepulchral abode
And I frantically wave my white flag
You were my girl, Cali, the only animal I claim that we've had
You were a hybrid, panther/lion with that mane and your fur all black

I've been working, but not in their standardized way =
Struggling with a loving God and with hearing what He has to say
Ranking relationships, sitting on the dock of the bay
But the fact that He Called to me and Made me hear are both testaments of His Grace
Qualifications are based in others' prerequisite expectations
But what is credibility if not pain made into relations?

8/10/18
My ego's at a zero, self-esteem is highly down. Anxiety's suppressing me, I didn't see till now. Acting like I'm over all these things I write about. My fear of the future is pinning me to the ground. So, I guess while I'm down here I'll take a look around. So long little buddy; let me know how I turn out.

8/19/18

The Blood
That Blood
Waterboard me in Blood

This Blood
Rejuvenates me from the things
I have done

8/20/18

Remember, Oh, My Soul, the prodigal was always the son.

2/25/18 – 26/18

On John 11:1-44

Picture with me if you can, my father's friend; a man I called Mr. Lazarus, had died of illness. We had been there in the duration leading to his passing and had joined in the weeping of his sisters and family. We were there when they wrapped his body with linen strips and adorned him with sweet aromas. We ourselves carried his limp body to a cave outside of Bethany. And we were among those who sealed the cave door by rolling a large stone in front of the entrance. We returned to the sister's home and grieved with them there.

Four days after his death, we received word that the teacher Jesus and his disciples were coming to the tomb shortly. This was shocking news to us all for we had sent the news of his illness long ago. So Martha went out to meet the master on his approach, but we remained with Mary in the house. In a few hours, Martha returned and took Mary aside, but I heard her say, "The Teacher is here and is calling for you." After this Mary left the house in a hurry, and we followed her, supposing that she was going to the tomb. But we followed her to where Jesus was and found her weeping at His feet saying, "Lord, if you had been here, my brother would not have died."

Seeing her and we who had followed her mourning, He was moved and asked, "Where have you laid him?"

We replied, "Lord, come and see."

As we walked, we could see Jesus weeping. Some of our group said, "See how he loved him." But most of us questioned, "Could not he who opened the eyes of the blind man also have kept this man from dying?"

When we came to the tomb Jesus said, "Take away the stone."

Martha told him, "Lord, by this time there will be an odor, for he has been dead four days."

Yet Jesus responded to her, "Did I not tell you that if you believed you would see the glory of God?" After this, we removed the stone, and as Martha had suggested, we were blasted by the cold stench of our friend's corpse. We stood away and watched as Jesus lifted His eyes heavenward and said, "Father, I thank you that you have heard me. I knew that you always hear me, but I said this on account of the people standing around, that they may believe that you sent me." After speaking these words to the sky, He cried out in a loud voice, "Lazarus, come out."

I peered into the dark tunnel expectantly. I wondered if the man I had heard so much about could raise this man I knew so well from his grave. For there was not even a hint of doubt within us of his death. I had seen his painful last breaths, and I had watched his body become pale as his blood ceased its circuit and circulation. I had seen and carried his rigid frame, and I had been struck with the feeling of someone I knew whose life had been pulled from their earthly body. I had felt the weirdness in my chest and compression of my stomach when I looked upon that being. Now I beheld something emerging from the tomb! That same figure I had last seen laying forever immovable in the cave was staggering his way into the daylight! What a glorious, ghastly sight! The joy of our friend's return was intertwined with the horror of that grave's resident rising again! In that exact moment, I believed all that this Teacher had said and done. I needed nothing more than to watch a man I had recently buried pass back through the door to which he was forever sentenced.

Jesus commanded, "Unbind him, and let him go." And that we did.

Songs- from 2015

Without eternity, it all amounts to vanity, these words are just grammary, I don't want you to trust me if

I don't have infinity in mind, I can try to find my life, inside of my mind

But I've tried to no avail, I can fly, and I can sail, so long as I'm on the trail that leads me home

Lies

seiL

Help me determine what is real

Help me to unearth the beginning of the seil

– Why is it that I, feel more alive, when I am alone and when I cry? We know that we should say, tomorrow will be better than today, but we always fall prey to the lies

– I think the difference between me and other victims is I recognize behind the lies is a pair of expectant eyes

– I happen to know that on his throne of broken homes he weaves a net to catch the things that are meant to make you a permanent addition to the life you live in why can't you see

– this opportunity to show that you survived being deceived

– so now you know that you can always take control of your emotions go and show them so that they can........

– I know how easy it is to be deceived – We fall into this every day – I know how it feels – Lies are supposed to seem real – But you can always escape the seil

Mine Mind

\\\\\\\\\\\\\\\\\\

The exact moment
I awaken in the morning
My thoughts are soaring
In the sky like a plane
Like the rumbling waves on the California cliffs
They are roaring
Not since 7 have I thought something was boring
Even in the sublime I'm admiring
Finding deeper meaning lying inside of finer things
I might find myself mining
Dynamiting mightily
Lining the mine

Figure 5. My mind

Of the meaning
Of Life
It's fine to say my mine's full
You could say I'm mindful
Diving in these lines
Then rising till I'm flying
Climbing to such heights
Now I'm gliding
Spiraling and declining
Towards an island
Where I'm lying
And reclining
Wallowing in shallow water
Just watching the sun
Shining
What I'm trying to say
In a creative way
Is my brain plays these games
Making these new worlds and places
Racing along through these made-up
Spinoffs I'm just chasing
Sanity, I know he's
Hiding around here somewhere
But whatever, I'll catch him later
Hey what's that?!
Oh yeah, it's another recollection from my past
How did I forget that one?
Just add it to the stack
At times it's a bit worrisome how much I can recall
Memories like mental hemorrhaging seeping

Before my eyes.
I don't like this part!
That's why I blocked it out
A long time ago
Why's it come to haunt me now?
Good Lord, I am so restrained by this pen
Here's the gist =
I know this way my brain goes is a gift
It's called a think-tank and the only catch with it's this =
If it's not properly directed the result is disastrous
No, we can't coexist
Not even my penis can I resist
At times my mind makes me cease and desist
Then at others I'll fight back and persist
But the persistence must consistently be consistent
Cause incidentally I always think consequentially,
Regarding lofty and lovely thinking
After the limits I have to translate these feelings
Conceptions, creations, inferences into the words worth your reading
Thus, I received a seeing is believing policy
So, I'm far from being a prodigy at any one thing
And if you're looking for me right now
The college is where I'll be
Not at USC so UC
Just an exec
Mastering ceremonies
Hosted in hall Oconee
Working on my future so
One day I'll be free

To settle down and earn allowance
For jotting down prophecies
Balance in all, so my thoughts fall between
Future and past
Cause that's where the present ought to be
I'll keep working out the kinks
Steering me and people to find that which we seek
Thank you for tuning in to this session on how I think
//////////////////////////////////////
This message was brought to you by
Me

9/12/18
It's always easier to say "($*)#*$ you" than "will you forgive me?"

9/18/18 - 9/20/18

"Where I Wish to Place"

Ok, I'm getting tired of games
I'm talking to the world as if
I can make a change
But the reality is that all that I write
Sounds the same
Not only that but in actuality it's lame
I don't want to come and go
I want to have shown up and stayed
I want to feel like every lyric's
Meant to be on this page
I want the people that just won't say it
But are choking from the pain
To find what God has given

And learn how to be saved
But before I do that
I guess it's time to reflect
Because the more I introspect = the more complex
That it gets
Even now I'm nervous, will this
All be a catastrophe?
What if I give this work my all
And what if they still laugh at me?
Night writing is where I feel like I belong
Trying to bring my pen to the speed
My brain travels is where I'm home
I know my purpose
And I have my hopes
That I can translate that meaning
Into a narrative that free flows
Straight from my spirit to
Hearers and readers via my mental lobes
I've got this calling, appalling as it may be,
That I could make a difference, explaining what has
saved me
And the reason why is that I've visited
Some of the places people have been living in
But because God delivered me, those people think I
never did
On the contrary, I'm familiar as a family member
That's why I can understand better than most
Seeing myself as a double agent
No one ever suspects the host

Look, the issues everybody's facing
I take them as personal
Why, one may wonder?
Because I'm a person and my Lord
Informed me I'm a servant of all
"All" doesn't appear to have exceptions
So, my edifice and prejudice must
Be switched with blessings
Regardless of bloodline, status, pigment, religion...
On goes the list of categories
But organizing differences categorically
Is laborious
And this is 2k18 and it's all about sorting
Our interests compared to others' as more important
Unless of course, someone agrees with yours
It is abhorrent
Sometimes I want to forfeit
But, tonight, I'm kicking the door in
This rain of terror on me has been pouring
And I'm tired of the enticements I know they have been luring
Me right back to that family of wacked maniacs to
which I'd alluded
Where am I going? Not a clue
All I really want to do
Is revisit these pages
After I go through some phases
And realize
These things I've privatized
Have the ability to be ageless

And if I remain faceless
It's better than being nameless
I hope this mood never changes
I doubt I'll be in the races
If I do, I hope I'm placeless
As long as I'm in His Graces
I know it's where I'll be safest
A modern-day Jeremiah
Spreading truth without any stages
Never making a difference
And never receiving praises

9/19/18

It could just be me, but I've seemed to be sidetracked- Just got handed my ($*)#*$- Think I need an ice pack- I just want to fight back- the fear, I don't like that- the point it's applied at- is where I can't hide facts- like a popped life raft- I'm drowning inside, trapped- in English confides clapped- in language irons I'm wrapped- flat-earth-like crap- off the edge of thy map- and it's high time that- I climbed right back- upon the right track- found a little flight path- covering the price match- proud that I can buy that- trying not to write trash- Aye! Snap!- Just checked where the time's at- My boo is waiting, what a sly cat- now commencing with our face-time chat.....

92118 – 92618
If I ever matter, the reason is my upbringing
Don't trust what you're reading
Technically, I am cheating
Can't believe what I'm seeing
Me's what privilege is breeding
This isn't meant for healing
I am raising the ceiling
This message is for heeding

Good Lord, is this what it has come to?

I feel it's a travesty! – To be harassed a person only has to be – of a certain colorant, it is sad to see – God allowed me and my family to live through tragedy – Now we just add it to the baggage, we – Would rather see His Spirit's Fruits fully ripe than souring – My parents' tales are far more empowering – but you get the pleasure to hear from their kid in his room = primarily cowering – and how his rise to power began with remolding – Finding out what the world has been withholding – Knowledge of good and evil, now that's what's called controlling – So, I'm told I won't ever make it because I didn't have a rough enough beginning – I suppose not, if I must keep up with your standards of goodwill and sinning – So what now? "what if this cracker, mother lover shows us up? – sucking our fun and chucking our blunts – summoning a ruckus and trusts our fans to shun us – once they unplug their crutches and retrain" – all of our lives, guys, it's not that hard to deviate – from what the world's relaying, that He may alleviate – the only difficulty's learning to live beyond the pain – and believe me, when it comes to this boat, I'm in the same – But now I'm told that about my color I should be ashamed – Passing down old grudges, and now I'm the one to blame – I promise I'll plead forgiveness, help me not make those mistakes – Just don't trample me when I acknowledge accidents I make – Don't you dare reverse the scales and become the people you hate.

10/2/18

'Tis a truly beauty-filled experience when two altogether different persons differentiated in color, education, heritage, levels of wealth, and separate cultural and regional influences are capable of possessing parallel thought processes resulting from analogical decisions enacted through relatively compact time durations jointed by adolescent mindsets. Such a situation seems far too improbable to have occurred by happenstance.

10/7/18

Wow, awe-filled, today's been a day full of raw thrills
Seeing and rethinking the balance between
Selling all-out and simply inspiring
I'm searching and working for an exact average = mean
The Bible belt's all that keeps in this obesity
Me and my buddy Kaylen been looking like Pair of Kings
God removed Mikayla, so I'm chasing down some dreams
Super speed like I'm SONIC along the way gathering rings

9/19/18 (4-22-21)

I'm feeling like I'm observing a proverbial Kentucky Derby.
Forming a union with the teamsters and the clergy.

I don't know why, but the words just won't free flow today. Please, LORD, I'm eagerly and expectantly pleading for your interceding to seed me and reap me with yourself into something worth reading.

10/10/18
Could it be I get some security stemming from my stockpiles of secrecy? The more I secrete, the more it cements – No, the more it concretes what I'm destined to be – I don't just get my path, destiny must have me – Looking at practicality first feels full of fallacy, especially with a tendency such as mine to dissect and misstep, I no rep myself when a day in its entirety passes me by with no contemplation of after we die – Because with that catalyst react all those infinities – And knowing which ones to pursue takes some ingenuity – That's why I take faith in my stride and it's why my heart-work gives me pride – But to me I can't be honest lest I have something to hide

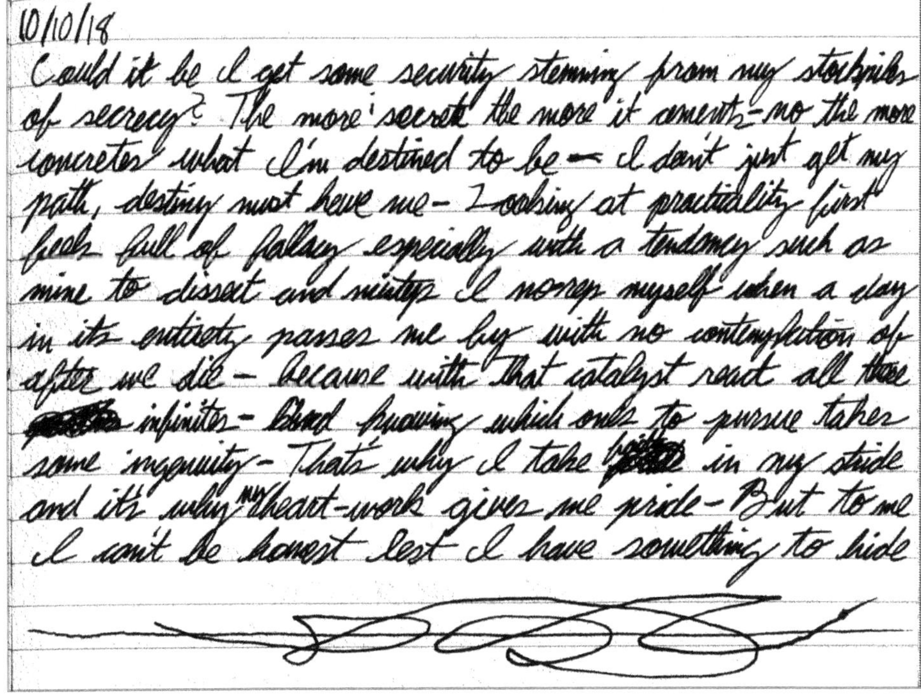
10/10/18
Could it be I get some security stemming from my stockpiles
of secrecy? The more secrete the more it cements – no the more
concretes what I'm destined to be – I don't just get my
path, destiny must have me – Looking at practicality first
feels full of fallacy especially with a tendency such as
mine to dissect and misstep I norep myself when a day
in its entirety passes me by with no contemplation of
after we die – Because with that catalyst react all those
infinities – And knowing which ones to pursue takes
some ingenuity – That's why I take faith in my stride
and it's why my heart-work gives me pride – But to me
I can't be honest lest I have something to hide

Figure 6. Stockpiles

10/15/18

Outlier

"What God brings together, let no man separate."
Exclusive to marriage? We won't differentiate
A recently received revelation revealed to me such a case
Please inflate your mind as I begin to explain...
Picture little youngins growing and going through phases
One hardly moves and the other travels the states it's
Incredible both would end up visiting the exact same mental places
They both seem to be developing equal intellectual traits
And eventually they attend a class on the same date
Immediately philosophies and theories start to take shape
Never a doubt they were brought together by far more than fate
Welded and melded together as one mind through one faith
Unsatisfied and desiring to inspire change
We will never fit in because we will hallow His Name

I fit in as much as a cardinal at a carnival
Called upon by a calling I sought and saw a long time ago
Collecting all my God and thoughts have allotted me
But I'm not yet scholarly enough for a following
Can't be shoddy when I'm offering all my products =
Quality more than quantity + also logic > profit =
This is my unique selling proposition
This is just a consequence of my not copying
I'm just chronically and chronologically chronicling
While everyone else is shopping
The only thing I'm afraid of is if I may end up flopping

Tho if writing becomes the cause of my success it won't be shocking
Not hoping to be topping any charts
All I want to do is just carry-on mopping stars
Calling card says stellar janitor...
That's what is hard of never being a part =
Alone you get battle charred yet your war scars
Are discarded
Returning from altercations to have your victories disregarded
But it's the normal that always soften
And the uncommon who become solid
For once the average have caught on,
Oddballs by long shots have already started

This just in from the midst of the Conflicted:
We apologize for messing up the statistics
All we're doing's just not pursuing the public interests
Don't misinterpret, we don't classify as gifted
And that won't fly because one cannot be our limit
Ourselves are the only confides to which we're restricted
Yes, it will be difficult, and results will be pitiful
At the most just a thimbleful
Or an isthmus of inability to attempt a fitting description
Please forgive me once again for symbolism
What we've got cannot be fought for with fists, it
Equally cannot be bought off with richness
Seemingly it's twisted
Feelings of bliss are kindred
With senses of sickness
This within half a minute

Birth or by contrivance
We know within our difference
Our purposes are decrypted
And to decipher we're driven
Ending with us, His Children
Witnesses may get livid
Placing us in derision
When the full picture's given
They'd been wishing for different tickets
If you feel as if this is you, listed
We regretfully inform you that it isn't
In fact, you may well be a hindrance
To our cynics, we remind of strictness
We do our best and hope for fraudulents' desistance
Though they come in droves when to Lucifer they listen
They put on such great masquerades even to themselves they're Hidden
The joy of hope in you be found if you know something's missing
He waits like an ecstatic child to know what you'll elicit
Tho there's one decision, nothing happens in an instant
Faith's not timed but measured by the weight which will be lifted
Change is not made by majorities but the space in a division
Ethereal joy for all coming to this side of the schism
Existence becomes better the greater the shift in distance
To Elohim be praise and welcome _______ to the misfits!

Your Name Here

This work was meant to give a personal representation initially of what it's like being an "outlier," or outsider, or whatever you may prefer. The opening verse is descriptive of the friend and the events that first had me considering what being an outlier may be. The second verse was a type of summary of how this looks in my life, and how you can become a better and more real person and how the world won't even care and that will be ok. The third verse is incredibly special to me because it's just a hopeful representation of what an outlier will experience in life, and because I stayed up writing it till nearly 4 A.M.; so almost 6 hours steady on a cold night. It subtly explains that someone who follows God is already the biggest outlier in this world. But it's about how a lot of people just say they're unique and different because they "feel" that way, and that this is an inhibition to Truth permeation. True Outliers are those who are being sanctified and "set apart" by God because He is <u>renewing</u> and pulling us away from the world whilst we are still here. It also testifies to the fact that it's not always sheer numbers that can steer a bell-curve. If an outlier is outlandishly far out of the data range, they are able to pull the mean and median towards themselves.

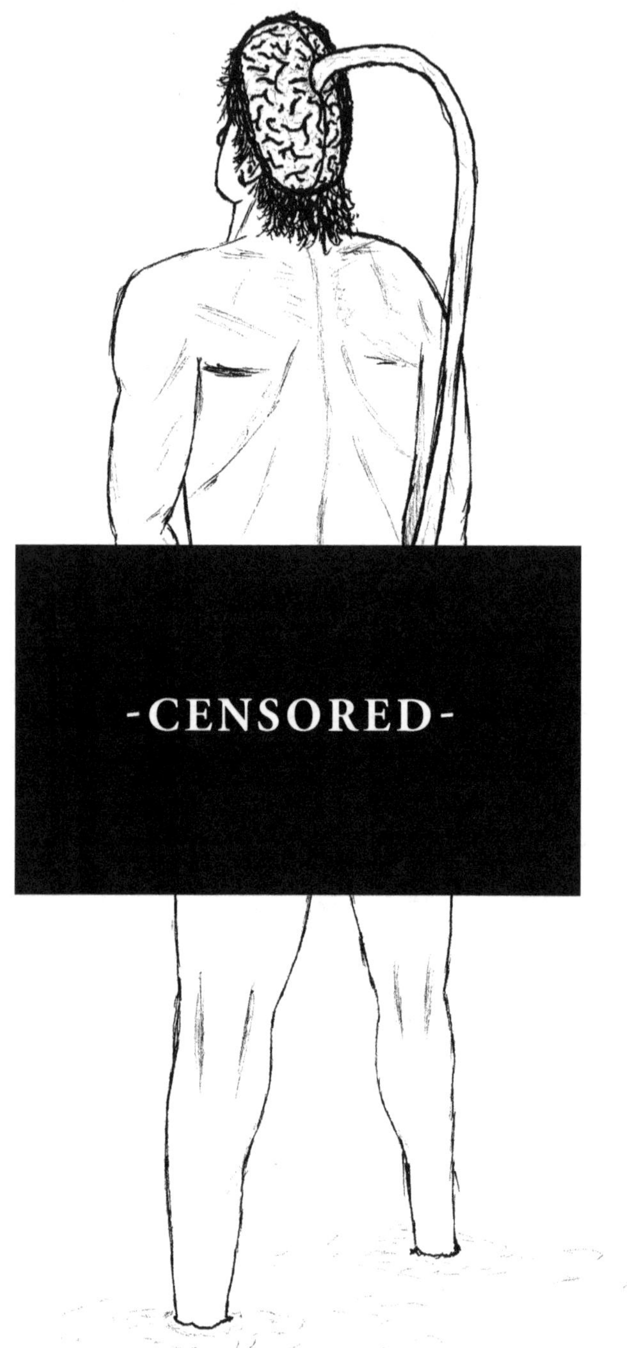

Figure 7. Sweat or smile [3]

I would rather make people sweat than smile.

10/18 – 22/18

I'm not up for rehearsing
But a bit of reestablishing
Has never been a bad thing
So, let's review,
1 deity = 3 entities
That's how to define a trinity
Triune is what we live
And when we die = we begin eternity
Trust me
I will not convince you to
Believe me
I just suggest that one is not observing if they can't see
Why He matters,
He means
We're all here for a reason
Entire lives reside on this
But the next stop's not appeasing
He Must Be Our Pinnacle
If we're to be purposeful
Pain = the other side of purpose
He = in the exact balance to us
Is perfect
Then everything which follows
Falls into perfect order
When Christ is the crest,
Then Life makes sense
All the way down =
The Waterfall Effect
The more truth divulged, the easier to distract
Thus, the need compounds for clarity to be exact
With that said, let us resume.........

11/19/18
The pressure's off when I realize it's not my life
It's His
And I never earned a thing
It's all a gift

10/24/18

BOOKS

Learning is a practice that is ever active if you let it. If I'm not learning, then I'm burning up this time I'm blessed with. This in mind, how do we learn? There's a variety of ways, but the most common is reading. Reading what? Books. With words. Especially with words we don't understand. They have been the primary investor in the transfer of knowledge for millennia. Though in the last half century, books have been in a conflict with music and movies. Movies and shows have become this generation's series and chronicles, and songs have gotten swapped for short stories and poetry. Though this isn't a detriment, it is unwise to throw out our volumes for the sake of digital data. Videos and things to stream are non-stop, going on with no end, without us, literally regardless. Books are inviting, awaiting our interest in them. This shift is an example of forgetting or disacknowledging the world's past and focusing solely on the future. If the human race runs headlong into the unknown without keeping in place our history, we are sure to make all new mistakes in the same exact way. Books, films, and tunes all use the same portion of the mind, and if they so choose, the same type of inspiration. And equally distributed through books and modern cinema and songs, there are those that offer little to no utility to peoples' lives. Here we must be discerning, as the preceding generations were with what to repudiate and which to revere.

Sensing incompleteness,
T. R. Edwards

"Writing is reaching inside of yourself and people and seeing what you find." – Dawn Greene

10/25 – 11/1/18

BOOKS pt. ii

You can say it's weird, sure
To feel the same about something never read
As a song never heard.
Over here the records of history are secured
In this zone are fictional depictions of realistic instances
Scripted to relocate the readers to non-existent incidents
No never an accident, everything's intended to influence
+ since the very first generation, humans have learned to document
To effect a state of equilibrium
One has to find what affects one and then measure them
Center your bubble then determine what their level's on
That's what I'm learning to balance = the records and the albums
And how it's the same talent of them in the past
Who passed down into the future the volumes that have to last
Just listen to the words which were molded from the same cast
Lying next to my head at night they somehow bring me repast
From underneath of their covers
So, excuse me
As I turn towards
Worlds
Galaxies
Universes
Realities
Inside
The pages I've got them
Trapped

1/16/19

Trenchant = Incisive or keen; caustic; vigorous; effective; clearly or sharply defined; clear-cut; distinct

So why should we fear Him?

He was the man we hope for today. He cared for the poor, sick, disabled, and the wronged. Likewise, He debated the religious, challenged the wealthy and condemned the hypocritic do-gooders. To all he extended forgiveness and gave each, every, and all equal value. His disciples believed so strongly in what He taught them, they shared it until their brutal deaths. One such follower named James informs us that <u>every good thing</u> is from Him. This means, of course, <u>every bad thing</u> is Not of Him. All those parts of life that are unjust and wrong and painful are not what He desires for us. John also reaffirms this by saying He did not send His son into the world to condemn but to save.

So why should we not fear Him?

He is as He says the Creator, so, also, He may be the Destroyer. All-knowing, all-powerful, all-present He claims. And we have turned our backs to Him and done those things He warned us not to. Since He is the supreme, prime judge, we are under His jurisdiction and sentence. For it would be unjust if He did not punish us, and He would not be good if He left us without the option of reconciliation.

So why should we fear Him?

He was the man we hope for today. He cared for the poor, sick, disabled,
and the wronged. Likewise, He debated the religious, challenged the wealthy
and condemned the hypocritic do-gooders. To all he extended forgiveness and gave each,
every, and all equal value. His disciples believed so strongly in what He taught them, they shared it until
their brutal deaths. One such follower named James informs us that <u>every good thing</u>
is Him. This means, of course, <u>every bad thing</u> is Not

....

Love ∞ Just

11/3/18

So Why should we fear Him?

He was the man we hope for today. He cared for the poor, sick, disabled, and the wronged. Likewise He debated the religious, challenged the wealthy, and condemned the wrongdoers. To all he extended forgiven and gave each, every, + all equal value. His disciples believed so strongly in what He taught them they shared it until their brutal deaths. One such follower nam James informs us that every good thing is from Him This means of course every bad thing is Not of Him All those parts of life that are unjust and wrong and painful are not what He desires for us. John also reaffirms this by saying He did not send His son into the world to condemn but to save.

So Why should we not fear Him?

He is as He says the Creator so also He may be the Destroyer. All-knowing, All-powerful, All-present He de And we have turned our backs to Him and done thos things He warned us not to. Since he is the prim judge, we are under His sentence. For it would be unj if He did not punish us, and He would not be goo if He left us without the choice to be reconciled.

So Why should we fear Him?

He was the man we hope for today. He cared for the poor, sick, disabled and the wronged. Likewise He debated the religious, challenged the wealthy and condemned the

Love Just

Figure 8. Just love

11/5 – 8/18

Mastur

The bait = it's real nice, in each shape and size
It takes what it likes, while it waits for your bite
Ooh it looks so good
But
The hook = is so sharp, with an eight-inch-long barb
It gets caught through your jaw; esophagus clogged
In your heart it gets lodged
And one day
You start to see, you're too far into this thing
You've shoveled and dug too deep, so you struggle and hope to flee
And that's when you see the string, it pulls tight, clenching your teeth
Then your gums start to bleed, and it rips into your cheeks
Then it yanks
You to the surface, you break through like a curtain
You take a glance around, the world is gone now
Welcome to the new realm that you have found
A hand clasps you strong
An eye examines long, contemplating where you belong
Chopped up for chum or thrown back and be done?
Either way we're the ones who gave him control
It's all fun and games till we may lose our soul
No point hiding when he's been sighted
He takes full credit afterwards for being behind it
Recall this lesson when next we fornicate
As we indulge there's a Mastur behind the Bait

11/9 – 12/18

That Night God Came Down

It was one Christian, Christmas convention concerned with crowds and cliques and Gants. Took it outside where in the 40s my circulation abandoned my hands. Shelter I sought in the open gravel lot. Looked heavenward and started throwing questions to God. Then in the darkness it dawned on me. The stars dropped bombs wrought with knowledge so cosmically. The group inside that room acts like they're following, but truth be told, God's outdoors in the cold, in the very marrow of bones, catching the awe you're tossing him and chuckling at your hot breath at His consent. This moment was God sent. A star-lit sonnet revealed a general direction of purpose and I hopped on it…

11/12/18

Feeling like I'm living in an infinite intersection and all individual seconds represent a separate direction, so I question every choice with discretion as if it were a polyspectrum = indecisive, sure, tho it's precise and protective. I just choose to direct my life by the lens of multiperspectives.

<u>11/12 – 20/18 Just as valid 5/14/22</u>

Yo! Got the new kid on the block – cultivating his mental acres and reaping a Holy crop – not looking to get loaded, but a little cash in his pocket – all he wants to do is write but still he works and goes to college – lives higher than an addict cause he gets just how far he's fallen – his spiritual savior dug a grave and buried the anchor he was hauling – the chorus from the joyous ceremony blares from a lofty Walkman – his earthly savior still trying to get a hang of the calling – yet she's first pick when he encounters an issue for solving – she's the best cause she's not afraid to tell him to stop it – and he knows if he's not sold out she'll tell him to top it – both of them don't and don't want to be like who the crowd's following – they sink deeper, filling up while all else are shallow and hollowing – delivers messages God sends to him feeling a bit like a shock collar – that's why he doesn't need an alter ego – so he leggo his ego and sacrificed it at the altar – grad students convey his propensities are said to be of a scholar – he's got this crazy yearning = his works be worth a high dollar ------------------------

Yes, this kid resembles a brick to swallow

Life swooping in like a hawk on a rodent – he just sits there watching it go in slow motion – hoping for most doors to close and the right ones to open – his only fear is not really knowing, but trying with all his might only for it to all end up blowing – so much pain in his head that he's not up or down for showing – his classmate tells him he's such an optimist – he can't help but scoff since his feelings are hardly positive – believing one is that which they think so he thinks that which he's not – "A man so is he as he thinketh within his heart" – satisfied at home tho one time he'll go afar – winter gives off death to most, but he feels it's a heavenly start – he hopes his few friends test him even if all the rest were to bless him – loves hearing advice and knowing he already learned the lesson – so when grandma said she'd been worried = had trouble the smile suppressing —- At the core, he loves to uncover life – And he says he'll be happy if those who know him are sure to find

In everything he did, he assured God's glorified.

11/12/18

Adolescence
Adult essence

Some people are so excited to be here. I'm worrying over what I get to take and what I'm supposed to leave behind. Will I grow to be old or be kind? Now, I can play pretend better than when I was 9. All those props and tricks for my own movies are within arm's reach. Only thing I'm lacking are the numbers of people who won't think me insane if I run around shouting and making my SFX. Getting nervous that the spotlight's about to turn and illuminate me. And I'm still embarrassed I asked for Legos on my 18th.

Anyway, my adolescence is turning into adult essence. I'm supposed to put aside my mess-ups and treasure my many blessings. God is showing me the growing process. Goodbye to the many few who took a large piece of me with them. Leaving by different trails, some I'll never see again. Your memorials are permanent, but I must make space for the newcomers to my heart. My parents were once unavoidable, but now all I want is eternal 7 o'clock; A.M. or P.M. = Wheel of Fortune or Fox. You two are incredible, and I never tell you enough. My favorite, every moment I savor it. Every second we pack away makes a brand- new relationship. Those who will go soon, don't let me a moment lose. I love you, and there's nothing else to Dawn upon. And finally, God, who's actually first, but he gets it. Please help me and speak to me that I'll listen. Make me need to know to love for YOU to be my desire. Whittle and kill off this wretch and make him something higher. I know you want me down here to share your message, just give me the verbals to always be effective (exactly like that).

Goodbye kid. It was an adventure to grow with you.

Farewell friend. I pray of God's Blessing For New.

11/13/18
I'm wishing to make a living
in an industry
This world is all but forgetting.

11/15/18
When He said, "truly truly," He dually exuded truth.
An excerpt from this date contained the first mention of an invaluable ideology of mine =

"I just feel to write is when God's finally smiling"
This has resonated and reverberated with few.

Figure 9. Cross the line

bad meat

I am growing weary
Of what people are throwing me
No exclusions
Including what they say's right
Sadly
But too many times
I've held my nose
And closed my eyes
Too much I sank my teeth inside
Bad Meat

True that
where the truth's at
isn't new wrapped
in a suit jacket
it's blue, black
with a bruised back
surrounded by sewer rats
and abused cats
oozing yak
juice that
makes you have
to gag
-
But change the camera angle.
With a little finagling we can make a hag look like an angel.
We would all assuredly be horrified if we saw all the things
that we glorify when they haven't been pornified.
For this reason, even more am I
Becoming a fan of plants, but by that I mean the floral kind.
Because they give the prime, perfect example for a life.
Blooming and proving through all its beauty we're sure to die.

11/21/18

What if I'm sufficient alone, I just won't try so I won't know?

11/21 - 22/18 Convos with our Heroes

If you could follow your heroes of the present,
What if you wanted no resemblance?
If you could encounter your heroes from the past,
What sort of questions would you ask?
If of their answers you'd have no clue,
Then ask yourself why do they inspire you?
If of your reply you're not quite sure,
Then what did they become your heroes for?
If someone else chose your hero to be,
Why did you succumb to your society?
If you realize you'd been duped by the hive,
On whom next to follow, will you please decide?

11/22/18

If you really want to know about someone, talk to the people who have known them the longest.

December 1st Now 2018

...Don't want to die now, just want to sign out = play around on the outside until the timeout...

12/6/18

Dredge me of my folly – Refund me for a hobby
Kinda sloppy but it throws a curve like it's a Rawling
Options popping up just delaying me from embarking
Offers may be alluring but then after they look like coffins
Pressure that's "not being injected" is commandeering my content – it's closing my tracheal brain passages, syllables transfer in pain days – I want exports shutting up the incomes – Influence

and money there has to be more than one – So I retreat into myself only to remember my self-destructive nature – And then I collapse in His River of Peace – The more I collect the more the words become cheap – I crave His reparation, that's why I started this thing – Father, help me retrieve all the Life that you bring
In the beyond unlikely case of this occurrence, I, now, on December 7th, 2018, at 11:15 A.M., plead that any aggrandizement of my work be entirely redirected to my Initiator.

Sincere Thanks,
Timothy

12/7/18 –

Fen (Quagmire)

Literally it's marshy almost all across the town
Humidity enveloped me right when I'd open the door
The stench of sweaty swampland was my morning aroma
The toxic people seemed like they loved being stuck in pluff mud
Contentment where I'd rested was a trend I wouldn't fall in
My investment in intellect surpassed the holders I came across
Progress lost the election and construction distracted attraction
Poverty started to lolly and privileged worthy of gagging
Insecurity lent equality so grouping followed suit
Plants important whereas work thought of as scant
The Holy Ghost still awaits His invite to that church
Children pick up depression like a hobby holding it tight
Drudgingly days are expended with variance frowned upon
Attempting to uproot displays the muck that holds so fast
Still, it will be nice to visit from time to time
I just bash it out of habit because it took more than it gives
But it's a set-piece of my story = that gory, whorred shore

- 2/28/19

I find that when I die, the endless hole inside my skull will be turned inside out to form a mount erasing doubts...

Figure 10. The endless whole

12/8/18
SouthBound
I'm headed to my second home
But it won't be real till we're alone
Most don't like "the parents," I feel bad for them
They help me to eradicate my mental phlegm
Thousands of people I encounter on the way
Not one distracts me from the look upon her face
I awe at the splendor of the spectrum in the sky
But it's elementary when relative to her eyes
I love my parents and I hate saying goodbye
But her embrace is what makes my heart start to cry
Less than an hour till I commence my winter break
Spending it in biessence, I know there's no better way

On the plane to Destin/Fort Walton, Miss Deborah T. told me to write down that she knew that I felt lost in a wilderness, and I was finding my way out. She believed I was chosen for a calling which would soon come my way. She hastened to explain to me she was no fortune teller, she just knew as soon as she saw me. She said that one day when I've accomplished my calling, I would remember that lady on the plane who believed I was destined for something incredible. This I am definitely sure to do.

12/21/18
Maybe this is all my downfall
Maybe It's
Jesus who's hiding me
Holy Spirit inside of me
And God I try to be
But somehow, I want Satan guiding me?
Sometimes during our pursuit to be different, we neglect becoming better.

12/22/18

L I M B O

I love your face in person
Months expectant of these days
Now I'm in dire need of a sermon
Before the visit ends without trace

Big questions block our view recently
We never found it hard to land a topic
Now we need something to defibrillate vehemently
A technique to pop this back into socket

Long term is the target, I'm scoping in on the 10's
The freedom is amazing, tho, the fear lurks right behind
In this moment, Lord, I pray of your calm to send
And bestow on us your foresight so we enjoy when we rewind

12/27/18 – 1/3/19

Candy Canes in Clemson

Christmas has passed
Cold winds take a pause
As if they were cued
Just as we start to walk
Through moments alone
Blessed euphoria thaws
How your cheeks lift
When I crank the car
Stroll through academia
Yet imposters we're not
Winter rays collapse

\+ Nude branches blot
Leaves left litter streets
Crackle when we trod
Creaky benches enact
Bases whilst we rob
Smiles laced our faces
Drives hosted by DJ Jon
Discoveries unearthed together
Are better when are not sought
All which we're left to say is
We want to go back as soon as we've gone

1/7/19 – 1/15/19 <u>Wondering Walks at Woodfield</u>

Across the thoroughfare
The drive winds West
Until uphill it unfolds

Resting atop the rise
The mansion glances down
Its slope unfurls as a scroll

Segmented in level sections
The street cascades to the lane
Each level we seek to know

We re-appreciate
The estate's lasting legacy
Brushing leaves from the stone

Hopes catching a spark
The ground might be ours

Our dreams increase as we stroll
Plans blazing a trail
The route caught in curiosity
Practically planting a goal

Swigging in living wings
The innkeeper sits in his richness, with us
Pleased at his being dethroned

When we're witness to privilege
The realization is evidenced
Higher standards to uphold

Those with less learn more
The need for sharing
With them supposedly below

Though oftentimes
The necessity for seclusion
Reclusive as if Thoreau

Forbid if a day comes
The imagination stores dust
This the dream which we chose

As well we deposit it in
The stars to remain
Up till it's our own

In spite of confusion
The truth's steadfast
Holding the other is home

1/9/19 On 12/30/18

Day of Joy	Day of Pain
Wedding Vows	Departing Planes
Piano Songs	Intercoms
In a Throng	Only One
Seems too Long	Already Gone
Too sad to sob	5/13/19 Overlooked Fraud
Plans to fawn	None to lean on

You're gonna remember me how you want to remember me

– inevitably, positive or negatively

– if tremendously, trust me I'm fine and I've entered this contest competitively

– Hot headedly? I will agree, I deserved to be dealt with so heavily

– yet, inversely, He coerced me by His mercy

– And, firstly, I learn more conversely

– But thirdly, if you're settled in treble levelment then you're treading in blessed detriment

– So sentiment, you've probably bled too much to be truculent

– I don't even know what I meant

– Just pondering what messages I have already sent

10/7/17 – 11/2/17

THE HOLLOWING MAN

Aye, him. The devious Charles Stettmier. Charles Alexander Stettmier that is. A man of primarily Dutch ancestry with a mind as cunning as they come. Oh, you would probably overlook him if you walked him by. He is a rather smaller gentleman; quite thin, with a healthy shock of grey-white hair. He is in brilliant shape, considering his age, and his mental capacities are in the peak of their prime, directly corresponding to his profession. He keeps to his habits while still being sociable and seeking humor. But his eyes, though; oh, his eyes: ancient as if they'd been connived centuries before himself. They were one of those misplaced pairs, living apart and confined to that bodily bone cage. Somehow you just knew; if you shared their stare, they had seen too much and imagined still more.

Because of his employment, though he'd retired years preceding, he could truly splendor amongst his successes. Grounds and a home, fitted for one much lowlier than he, was where he addressed himself. A respectable home yet not exceeding one's need, and a myriad of worlds full of spectacle resting inside the skull, this the living ideal of our dastardly man. His habiliment speaks humbly though he could adorn himself as a lord.

But his job, of course, yes, his job. Mr. Stettmier is a man of a multitude of surgeries. He studied incisions and observed many transplants. Years did he delve into the surgical world, and then he began his illustrious profession. Times over and again was he renowned for his career of careful treatment within the soft human encasement. Such a collection of times and what a number of areas, few as much as him understand the human body. He was oh-so familiar with the inner and outer workings of the soul's present physical state. Most would say he enjoyed this employment. Very much indeed.

It could be supposed that it all began many years after his well-earned yet early retirement, when he started the involuntary hand movements. There would be times he would become aware of his fingers moving in that melodic, methodic way they had so many times before. Such as soldiers' engrained triggering responses or the unconscious memorization of musicians, as would Mr. Stettmier preform those surgical verses upon thin air. Though he tried and he tried, those habits within his hands could not be stopped. If anything, they became more frequent, expelling themselves at every subconscious susceptibility. My, but too soon, these subtle reactions followed him inside his slumber. And oh! Then too quickly, the gruesome sights returned steadily to that poor man's scavenging sensibilities.

We cannot pretend to fathom what those years of mobile practice and then years of sedentary inactivity engendered in the midst of that man's psychosis. If there is one primary source available to change a human's course of thought, it is unrestricted and uninhibited time. Time alone amidst endangering thoughts can bring either the unbelievable progression or the unexplainable downfall of one's brain's capabilities. When a highly active and majorly educated mind is left in immobility and solitude for too long of a time, it will either rise and achieve or dip and begin to scheme. And whichever of those options conquers the other, it will invariably and furthermore steer the thought patterns and actions of the individual. If only our example had the strength or acumen to succeed and ascend past such mental fray. And as with any reduction of natural attitudes, he, oh-so-slowly declined. Years, dear friend, years did it creep upon him. So unnoticeable 'twas. This sickness, this disease, nay! This esoteric epidemic overtook the poor creature cell by disheartened cell. One might say this resembled a tiger, awaiting to pounce on his fright-filled being. Yet there was no need for the striped predator to lunge. For by years made of seconds made of stillness, the man stared into those ever-seeking eyes, and the enemy took the victory, not by a sudden attack, but by decaying the defenseless internal strongholds moment by horrendous moment. Molecule by molecule. The overcoming was accomplished not by the thrashing and slashing of bodily weaponry, but by the creeping, seething of inherence. Blood drop by drop. Infection of idea greeted the poisoning of time! Oh! The thought! Oh! The crawling decimation!

So unnoticeably did the infatuation return. Slower than imperceptible. Envision years, friend. For an unbeknownst amount of years these diligent, vile thoughts gained ground. His daily routines began to vary, as he spent more time in his recollections than his aspirations. Stettmier started to relive his procedures to the utmost that his memory could afford. There remains to be constructed a measurement of how gradual such a rottenness could accumulate.

Though, still, it was too soon. Death is the soonest that lust should be accomplished. Lust, yes. After so much time reimagining his old practices, he, of course, wished for more. How could he return, he dreamt; what would the practicing surgeons think of him, he wondered. Would they view him simply as a curious soul, wishing to be kept up to date on modern doctoral issues and procedures? What if they perceived him as a bloodthirsty man? An individual who derived a fulfillment from the peculiar fascination of being an onlooker to a living being's inner components. That would be outrageous! May it never be! How dreadful a truth that would comprise!

What was actually occurring at the nucleus of the deception? Was it the strange, fickle desire already described? How sincerely harmless was that? All he wanted was to look upon one more human beneath the skin. Simply a whim. There dwelt within him a wish. Nay. There was within him a desire. Nay! A longing, that's it! But perhaps... Could it be? He possessed a yearning! And what a haunting yearning!

Before too long a time, Stettmier had changed. Alterations arose though he still entirely remained the son of his parents. He grew trouble remembering the most simple tasks. He'd lie awake for so long into the night. No matter how engaging a moment was provided, he was distracted. The worst of it, however, was to be out in the world. Out amongst the rest of the creatures... the desire was easy to conceal, though it never was eradicated. But over time, that dreaded dastard, the longing resumed. He could not converse without wishing to see within the flesh of every human he saw! This was maddening to him! This brought him to the precipice of tears! Weeping as a child who comprehends they could never own something they want! You could venture the idea that he was tampering with insanity!

Oh, but he was not insane. What a condemning, defying term! This falsity is preposterous. Those who are "insane" are as fit as we; perhaps they've just taken one thought a little too far. We're not that far, dear friend. For Mr. Stettmier was as secure as the sense of sanity can be. The man, of course, knew that he could not dissect whomever he chose off of the street. He was fully aware of the disturbance. He was in no way insane as we would wish to deem him, but there still smoldered amidst him the gruesome pining – My, that pining.

Not insane, no. Though still that craving remained. Where could he release that swelling tension? In what manner could he expel his lustful passions? For the fantastical imaginings surpassed just one of his sense's abilities. He had progressed to not just wish to see such things, but to feel them – feel the heat. His fingers quivered in vain attempts to feel the blood floating through the vessels. His ears attuned themselves to detect the bass throb of a heart. His nostrils were accustomed to the aroma of uncovered tissue. He wanted so devoutly to sense the inside of a fully functioning homo sapien...

There was always one. He always had that singular individual who calmly awaited. One vessel had he until death overtook them both. Deep down, Mr. Stettmier knew he could always vivisect himself. Even this seemed a bit of an over-step, or a step towards the, shall we say, extra-sane. Surgical, personal excoriation. Bah! Foolishness! For it has been assured he was more than able to control himself.

If only he had. If only we hadn't the dismay of depicting otherwise. No, he instead derived his old tools, for they had not been stored too far from access. Nevertheless, the culmination of years on end; thoughts upon thoughts; the evolution of desire was funneled into particular, horrid moments.

He exposed his pale arm, the left to be exact. In some craze-riddled seconds he paused and breathed, and we shall not tire ourselves trying to imagine what occurred inside that soul's skull in that time. We shan't venture to understand those synapse's and movement's reasonings. What happened afterwards was too much for anyone apart from him to justify. Whatever went about in the brain was transferred to the sickening blade. It was forced into the skin, yet not too deep into the underlying filaments. The scalpel was pulled along until it had traversed half of the forearm. And this was repeated parallel to the first at the other end of the arm. Then the most shocking was effected; one perpendicular slice to join the two incisions. This quadrilateral shape traced the whole of the forearm, from the mid-arm bend to the start of the palm. Finally, came the terrific unveiling. He sublimely pulled back the thin epidermis. He beheld that which he'd dreamt of for so long a time. It would appear to any that he had discovered a forever-lost treasure. He discerned the steady convulsive blood passing to and fro through the arm. He identified, labeled the muscles, the tendons, the bones. He prodded them, moved them. He watched them writhe as he wriggled his fingers.

I do hope you can see how it came to this degree. No words could be written to explain why the last excerpt. Here is where it could more easily be accepted that Stettmier's sanity was in question. Though be assured of the contradictory, informed one!

Though quit there he did not. He for hours did these actions mentioned before, sane as they were. His calf did he slash! Then his thigh did he slice! But what drove him to proceed as he did? He extra-sanely, we suppose, cut the sinews of one muscle; one, he apparently deemed as unnecessary. After, he cut through the fibers of the base. How could a human then pull this flesh out! How could a person extricate such a thing from themselves! Out of every section, a portion was removed by him! There could be nothing worse than his mid-segment. He was forced to look in the mirror at those eyes all the same, and blatantly scarify his own abdomen and sever his own ribs! How terrible! It causes a cringe! How disgusting! What type of drive would go to such lengths or such depths?! What style of impulsion would ignore one's own conscience?! Oh! Just the thought! Oh! Simply the image! It radiates nausea! It tugs at our own sanity! Behold my ragged friends... the Hollowing Man!

2/4/19

2/4/19
It's been a minute - I'm questioning if I was ever really in it
half a month since I died, I'm just a remnant guy; please
quit me living - Back to role playing - my brain is having
a full-blown convo with itself I'm no mo head honcho
lost all control bye status quo moral compass swallowed
cause the magnetic field's hollow —— No I don't have
a clue what I mean - The words don't have to be unique
madness setting in like it's concrete - Something bearing
that resemblance is inching me towards malevolence - I
search in the words I've penned - can't find any relevance
each step is within a trance - Am I tempted by trends
You would look dumb in dreads - I love the word contrivance
Now I hate waking up - The nightmare rises with the
sun - Firstly the words were heaven sent -

Figure 11. Spiral

2/6/19

Sanctimony

Pride's defied me, so I'm hiding, try to find me, dark's behind me, fear's beside me, light is blinding, access denying, lies I'm fighting, more are lining, opponents sizing, me up shying, each more trying, but not complying. That literally sucked

^Over intercom^ #It seems the test subject is having difficulty believing all the truths he so recently was lost without# 8===>

The words, can't get a hold of 'em – in my skull's pandemonium – violent as water and sodium – these days I don't like my story, it's so heavy, doc, where's my DeLorean – Feels like these goods were sabotaged by the salesman who sold me 'em – deceitful business, trickery's what it takes to get to me – Now I'm stuck guessing which one of us was the phony – I guess it's me cause I'm flirting with sanctimony – Growing ill of sharing myself so I think I'll stick with aloning... Hold up... Heap blessings upon thee it's a mess in this event and I'm the only contestant – a non-experienced chemist whose reaction's effervescent – my pretense is to think I can escape depth – the next step's in question, my review has bred lessons,
I lost the directions to heaven, and now I'm obsessing – I've dragged out these sessions and now have no final message, bye ///"~:_*#we now return you to your regularly scheduled program......*

2/12/19

Sanctimonious (continued)

I celebrate the life I had more than the one I've got. I really feel betrayed, scared to take another shot. Withdrawals from a love I didn't know I was on. Just a few farewells left + now the hardest is gone. Steady on, the vitality is practically a habit as it's sad to be having difficulty grasping at the lack of words contracting me – plans found another man with a future –

she just left me with a mile wide suture – groggily I wander 'round as if in a stupor – succeed or fail I will still be a loser – without her I flounder – and figured it out in the shower = deadly and deathly loyal but to fewer by the hour = When someone or something is threatening them – I shatter their glass and segment them with shards – but this new enemy and weapen is sent – So I see there is no one to fight so then with myself I spar – I cannot fit it so I'll rip myself apart – I believe the words I bleed I just can't get myself to start – Inspiration here and far, but I'm needing more than a spark – Don't let me slide to where I'm all-feeling – This that one case for a price ceiling – Please keep me from equilibrium lest you'll be singing my requiem………… All this to say, when I'm face to face with complacence, He takes me to crazy places and waits till I break out of stasis. On this installment, His latest, in importance, it's guageless. With this hint I've been chastened === Greatness is Wasted in Havens

3/24/19

Red Eyes, Late nights, and saline blights
Byproducts of a brain quite
  Uninspired late

Migraines, Ocular and Faith blind
More frequent at the same time
  Love must take a break

I'll try, any to delay this plight
Wake up in a cage fight
  Keep the beast untamed

Rhyme and meter seem to waste lines
When I cannot train my-
  Self with what to pray

Compos mentis = Sane; mentally sound

Figure 12. Compos mentis

Aro/und/Then

Durdenesque

Can you feel the percussion rhythm of societal interactions? How much do you lick the rim of overspilling consumerism? Do you ride the ebb and flow of emotional discontinuity? Do you like your new cloth chains around your neck? Is the concrete more natural contacting your heels? Does the concept of true destitution make you more fearful than being a mean family member? Has the floor always felt like a consoling parent? Has advantageous advancement abruptly run out like blocked cheese through a grater? Sewer pipes are inviting, am I correct? Did repulsion retreat into seclusion? If she did, what did we decide to bribe her with? How high of a percentage will gas prices receive? When did clouds flee? Will the floorboards become the ceiling tiles of our caskets? How strong of adhesives comprise our minds? Is depravity not impracticable knowledge? Will sex in and of itself not criticize? Since when did acting metamorphose into the most commonplace, lowest-grossing career of these days? Did the Dark Ages just get a desk lamp? How is it that we have come to eat in the same manner as our animals? Are we only friends with people who think we're always right? Have we truly experienced our mental capacity if we've never sweat while motionless? Are we held responsible for the misdeeds within our dreams? What is the perfect mode of reclination? Why does Velcro have a more useful life estimate than humans? So, what makes status the hierarchy of social acceptance? Why do we not acknowledge that conveyor belt called time that carries our meat to our designated cans?

2/22 – 3/28/19

Slam

Birthed with firm grips on resilience – To the curb, we're cursed by the millions – We mature by a set of rules – Mostly molded by what's cultural – Question the crowd, counted out as residuals – But one day, we embrace, and we say it's okay just a test on our quest to become individuals – Testing, 1, 2, ... Can you hear me robots? – Come on, get your head out the box – Look afresh at the world for a second – Look anew at the life you've been blessed with – Don't go back in the past, just learn the lessons – Don't rummage what's coming, take the gift and be present – There are temporal and eternal, let's bisect... – Infinite is the one who created it – Many names, just one saves, we won't waste time by saying it – So we may be assured He gives every good thing – I got that from James 1:17 – But we told Him "no, thank you" and He let us be – True love is nothing if both are not free – And He tells us, Arms Opened "Please, come to me" – This puts me at risk, these words I believe – I just increased my likelihood of being killed on the street – but I trust in True Justice and Love must come from me – Cause by the t-i-m-e, now do you see? – We reside inside the temporal realm where we live, breathe, and bleed – As humans we abuse our responsibility, let freedom ring – So we yell and we hurt and we curse and we scream – And we use our "bad words" and we call people names – In that process become them: the people we hate – Minorities are silent and we're not quiet anymore – While we rant on the roof, who'd we fling to the floor? – Remember countries are comprised of people, so one is where to start – Don't just uphold symptoms, dig deep into the heart – Nothing ever gets done when we leave it at being offended – Time is forced to applaud if we establish a line and defend it – Only ourselves can teach us how to learn and the curve's circular taking turns with the worst then the lines will get blurred ending with reason rended – So let's be who we are, not find who we want to be – Let's together figure what's right and become who the world needs – Kiss emotions goodnight and wish them some sweet dreams – Balance is key, but which ways do we lean – Beyond the logic or more deep than feeling? – Either way, Fear of Him is where wisdom begins – And usually we remain inelastic because it's a truth we can't bend – So, our pride responds reminding us we've been through a lot – But if you've received any of this message, well done cause you didn't stop – And whether we like it or not, it's in His image we're wrought – This quick visit to life answers Why when He sits at the top – Actually it gets harder when you discover that which you've sought – Yet never will we regret it when we remember the cost

3/3/19
Who are you talking to? Me? You? You, Me, Who? Oh, You? You here too?! It's so good to see you dude!

3/7/19

Lucubrate = To work, write, or study laboriously especially at night

3/30 – 4/5/19

Premonotion

Come, let us dwell upon it
Scrutinizing these guys' content
They sure recite awe-worthy sonnets
Block critical comments
Outright causing colic
Pride won't satisfy
So, there's no time for pausing

Almost all have a homologous problem
Besides trying to tell us they're all in the top office
If we had their every breath and letter it still wouldn't be honest
Respect is best and mine is kept, gracias señor Chavez
Regret humility's dead when none know every one is in process
But those are the blind.
What of the received?
When I took advice
From a mother who's wise
She said, "Look around you,
They're dropping like flies."
So, should I even try?
To relay as a spy
Enemy messages
With this pen I ply
There should be no I!
Read daily to die!
Whate'er comes of it
Is no longer mine!
&
Gravity's tossed so I am to let go
Whether everyone receives or no one else knows
Let me see as my late brother Horatio
Every part of this life Be Well With My Soul

4/5-12/19

Apply myself to be trenchant
Instead get drafted as schizophrenic

Don't worry, it's just genetic
Jack passed in the institution they kept him

One minute, I'm king of the Celtics
In the next, draining your septic

Most times, be described as clement
Occasionally, my presence is dreaded

Alone, late in the A.M., I'm hectic
Yet sees any other, he's trepid

To some he's well-respected
To others, reputation's decrepit

Might help with why he's hesitant
Just missed testing the theory of severance

It's neat because he's his worst skeptic
So, he never does what he's expecting

Don't listen to him, it's listed with my blessings
Yeah, you think that now, but you won't in a second

4/11/19

Not the God of the Bible
Or the God of the Word
But the eternal first player
Who pressed start on the universe

4/12 – 5/18/19

TO THEM
THE FARTHEST

You all are just Dialectic, forgetting Nature and Ethics
It's tragic you stick to lyric, yet comedic you don't lead epics
Yes, your dictionary I've read and been over again
Remembering the memory every now and then
Instead when you went out of your way to implore us
"You all should bow down, follow, and adore us"
Bugattis and Lambos and you still can't afford us
"Worship of man's," not worded in my thesaurus
The more gets poured in the smorgasbord

The horde's sure to abhor
Not ominous, I am Not showing off
I'll just keep things moving like sorbitol
You have everything you want,
I have all I need,
The simple issue your wish missed is wants will
Never Cede
That even means when your platinum album's on repeat
No envy from me with no unique beliefs
Your occupation is shamming
We're getting sick of the antics
You're newest hit's second-handed
The mode you've chosen's pedantic
Most of you got your screws loose
When detonation ensued it blew your fuse
Karma checks the credibility while behind you the sparks shoot
Good luck looking for the good they're doing, ask anybody, it's proven
Impacts as atomic blasts react as in mushroom clouds
But even in Hiroshima the flames faded and fizzled out
So be grateful... little gift... Bow down... little gift 2x
Come at me
Your Bentley, your Audi, Dat Gucci, Versace
Wherever you're shopping has got carbon copies
I stick to ripped DC's practicing my ollies
Followed by Darlings, that Hook is a cod Smee!
So you pay for Rolex, I'll take the Timex
Checking my Codex, watch that cause it's priceless
I found the word garrulous
It's all I compare you with
Gargoyles, goblins, demogorgons, and dogs
You're villains, killing it, ending as demagogues
My whole goal is to be so unlike you
Laying hate and spreading waste, you're roaring like a Kaiju
Choruses and verses with less talent than a haiku
Hanging papers gained by trained rehearsals aren't an IQ
Streets still count as solid ground, I groveled from the bayou

We wanna be so indwelt we can't help but apply truth
My writers, my typers, my hypers, my vibers
My comrades whose time is best spent to decipher
I hope you believe what you say and aren't liars
Authenticity means more to me than being suppliers
For in that pursuit we remain always stirred
And hope rests with unsettled and willing to learn
But they play ring-around-the-rosy and the rosy's really hope
Even when they've fallen down the next go around won't be close
Large scope but you're aimless – messages are persuasive
Ignoring your crimes are heinous
We should be fine feeling invaded?
So with the lowliest I'll stay adjacent
If in the south, these works are the greatest
Then I would at any time remain uneducated
I beg of I Am, I am not your replacements
Now at the tops, you feel no need to chase it
New products each day can classify as complacence
Can't hide in a flask or a cask, it's encasement
I'd rather believe and be wrong than be faithless
Please do me this favor if it's for your living
Bring back that rawness you had in the beginning
We see the bickering, it's more fitting for children
It's not my place, I'm uncomfortable dissing
Yet I already do and to this you will listen
Diss tracks just distract and miss that commission
I'm a Child of God!
Be sure, be bored, or report me
Never think I want you veering towards me
Best isn't who you're destined but intended to be
If your influence depends on you that's no legacy
Preservation through winter's what makes evergreens
Sure, you're the farthest, but we're not too much apart
Mutual respect almost never led to harm
I pray for just one item you'll add to your cart
Instead of getting directions, the truth is where you start

4/12/19

"Be a Carver among the farmers" – Ted Edwards

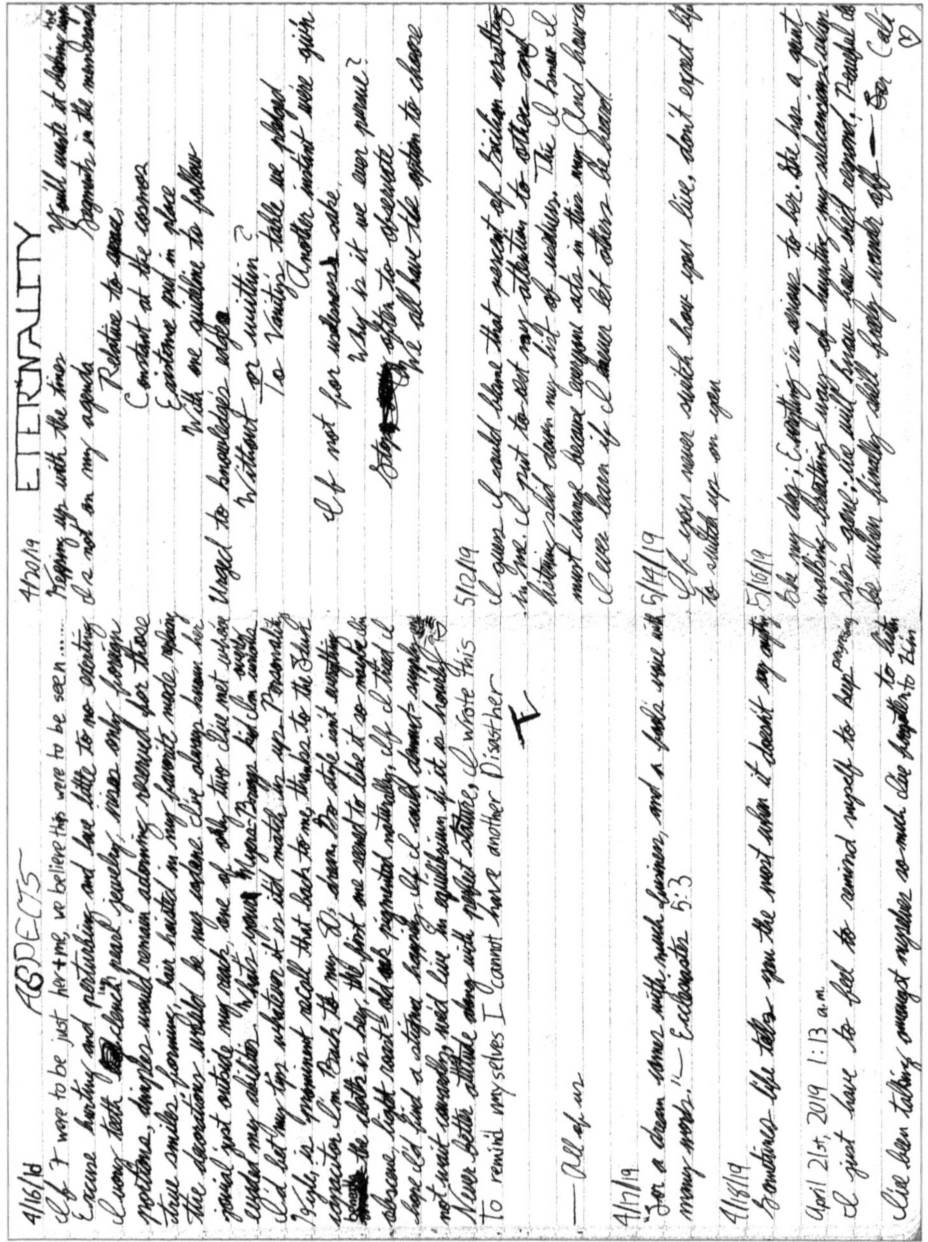

4/16/18 ASPECTS

If I were to be just her + me, we believe this were to be seen.....
Excuse hurting and perturbing and love little to no exerting
Ivory teeth clench pearl jewelry, [illegible] only foreign
portions, dimples would remain adorning reserved for those
true smiles forming, hair hoisted in my favorite mode, replacing
the decorations would be my [illegible]. I've always known her
jovial just outside my reach, one of only two I've met whose
[illegible] my abilities. What's your Myers-Briggs kid I'm overly curious
I'd bet my tips whatever it is it'd match us up. Personality
Kyle, is prominent recall that back to me, thanks to the [illegible]
capacitor I'm Back to my 80s dream. [illegible] style isn't everything
beneath the cloth is key, the first one seemed to like it so maybe I'm
obscene, light roast = old oak pigmented naturally, If I tried I
hope I'd find a stigma happily, If I could [illegible] supply [illegible]
not wait cowardly, we'd live in equilibrium if it is hourly
Never better attitude along with perfect stature, I wrote this
to remind myselves I cannot have another Disasther

— All of us

4/17/19
"For a dream comes with much business, and a fool's voice with
many words." — Ecclesiastes 5:3

4/18/19
Sometimes life tells you the most when it doesn't say anything

April 21st, 2019 1:13 a.m.
I just have to feel to remind myself to keep progressing
I've been talking amongst myselves so much I've forgotten to listen to Him

4/20/19 ETERNALITY

Keeping up with the times
Is not on my agenda
Relative to space,
Constant at the cosmos
Existence put in place
With one guideline to follow
Urged to knowledge's edge
Without or within?
To Vanity's table we pledged
Another instant we're given
If not for [illegible] sake,
Why is it we ever pursue?
often to observate
We all have the option to choose

You'll waste it checking the signs
Segments in the memoranda

5/12/19
I guess I could blame that percent of Sicilian [illegible]
in me. I put to rest my attention to others and
listening slid down my list of values. This I know I
must change because everyone acts in this way. And how could
I ever learn if I never let others be heard.

5/14/19
If you never switch how you live, don't expect life
to switch up on you

5/16/19
Like my dog; Everything is serious to her. She has a giant
walking, breathing way of haunting my subconscious when
she's gone; we will know how she'd respond. Peaceful she'll
be when finally she'll freely wander off — For Cali ♡

Figure 13. Aspects & eternality

4/16/19

ASPECTS

If it were to be just her + me, we believe this were to be seen........... Excuse hurting and perturbing and love's little to no exerting. Ivory teeth clenching pearl jewelry, irises only foreign portions, dimples would remain adorning, reserved for those true smiles forming, hair hoisted in my favorite mode, replacing the decorations would be my codeine. I've always known her jovial, just outside my reach, one of only two I've met who've evaded my ability. What's your Myers-Briggs, kid, I'm overly curious. I'd bet my tips, whate'er it is it'd match us up. Personality, Kyle, is prominent, recite that back to me. Thanks to the flux capacitor, I'm back to my 80's dream. So style isn't everything, beneath the skin is key. The first one seemed to like it so maybe I'm obscene, light roast = old oak pigmented naturally. If I tried, I hope I'd find a stigma happily. If I could demand = supply and not wait cowardly, we'd live in equilibrium if it be hourly. Lol. Never better attitude along with perfect stature, *I wrote this to remind myselves not to have another Disasther.*

- All of us

"For a dream comes with much business, and a fool's voice with many words." – Ecclesiastes 5:3

4/19/19

Ruminative Coping Style = Persistently focusing on how one feels without attempting to do anything about one's feelings

5/29/19

Eradicate death from a man... Oh, you can't? Then I'll trust the one whose uproots must supplant

5/15/19

If I keep it honest | If I keep it honest
I'll rebuke the sophists | He's burning my sin audit
If I keep it honest | If I keep it honest
I'll freeze in tropics | I'll eat at Red Robin
If I keep it honest | If I keep it honest
Time is harmless | I'll need electronics
If I keep it honest | If I keep it honest
No one will top it | I'm bombarded with topics
If I keep it honest | If I keep it honest
I'll disentangle bollix | I'll end what I started
If I keep it honest | If I keep it honest
I'll hand out colic | I'll never lack aweness
If I keep it honest | If I keep it honest
Like Brooklyn I'll dodge it | I will promote to phonics
If I keep it honest | If I keep it honest
I can't be stand-offish | I'll have to be guarded
But if I keep it honest, I will never be Godless

5/23/19

Captured, tortured, POW to hormones. KIA'd by the AID of a maid in a warzone. Put my sex life on an indefinite sabbatical. Trying to be refractory with no collateral. Slowing my role in this paddle boat. Now I just want to go where the cattle roam. No more whack a mole. Put on hold, cause that thing is retractable. I wanna get practical. Life that's changed like radical, just like David Platt had wrote.

But I'm glad it happened.

Glad to be inactive.

Actually I'm sad, wish I had subtracted that which I contracted. I would enact the passion, so attractive, made it a habit and acted up like a spastic. Haphazardly, in the action, I was gradually trashing my hypothalamus, bashing out my sagacity, and slashing off my capacity for potential orgasmic tenacity. Adamant, there's no better applicant. For within that happening, I've acquired the knack to unpack the packaging, added it to my bag and saddled it to my caddy's back. Can you hear the clacking of the shackles? They're latching themselves to our protoplasms by digital acrobatics amassing massive caches of data + adding stacks to the fractal strata casually hacking our backup and ravaging classic adages as well as the casualties wallowing like the Sadducees. This doesn't mean they're not distracting me. But I'm giving the performance of a lifetime acting out chastity. I'm preserving, I'm a servant, I'm a Maccabee. And we're ok with it, tho none of my past selfs clap for me.

5/30/19
I swear I love you all, but couldn't be an agnostic, I need a reason for objects, be ducking the noose of narcotics, my timeline acquired a blockage, obstacles r what I've gotten, I'm flying blind aeronautics, wishing to be more like Ogden, that's what will get me popping...
Thankful for negative comments, my purpose here's like a solvent

Summer 2019

LOVELORN

No FIFA, speed balling, Sonic Hedge-hogging, God made me
odd and uncommon, as was Solomon whose authored sagas
and proverbs were solid, he was wrought with knowledge but
lost it all to his concubines whilst unclogging his chakras...
That's why I'm fine as a Hobbit not governing Gondor or Rohan
The cost is comical, Calvin & Hobbes crossed with Foxtrot
Screw Aruba and the Bahamas
The bongos and the maracas
Erotic mambos and salsas
Knocking hollow piñatas
Thongs and popping tops just don't hit on my spot
Bungalows on the coast are simply too humid and hot
Leaving the city, Hawkins, not Dema, but watch the doggies

I'll take a secluded cottage in the Canadian Rockies
Hearth with dreams and memories, burning logs, and snow sprawling
I know she'd be sockless, legs crossed, baggy pajamas
Knowing for me she was chosen is what gets me oohing and aahing
So stop walking about with false confidence
You're uncomfortable, and it's obvious
Won't last long if all it is is provocative
Character first I compliment
Modesty's The accomplishment
Screw your clothes, it's the heart of it
The pursuit of good is worth honoring
Hope your days are long and prosperous
Receive Joy and <u>then</u> enjoy opulence
FOR

Playboy Station, it's not where Greatness is waiting – penetrating hotties across the nations = ladies' asphyxiation is aspiration's assassination – if that gets me elated, splatter my gray matter on pavement – I would appreciate if she had His admiration – I'd need her needs' abatement, baby let's find privation – We'll make biessence my vacation – each kiss worthy of standing ovations – If you'll bless me with silent gazes, I'll ask "honey, what's the occasion?" ------ kicked off a spinoff poem, I guess I'd better save it – sitting, considering my present situation – I love with love He gives me: pages upon pages – tho it's what I've been craving, been begging for no relation – I'd rather die of starvation than overcompensation – From what Jr.'s been telling me, guess I'm in need of straightening – Being a boy caucasian in this day and age can be dangerous – We get away with tax evasion – Every one of us is a rapist – I falsified the last 2 statements – I believe that my generation – Can give prejudice a replacement – "Wait, I thought this was going to be about love making?" – Yeah, my First Love wanted me to make this proclamation – My best and blessings from Him (no rhyme) and Amen

*Figure 14. Hartwork by Devin Eatman @DEVIN_ARTS_*

9-12-21 – *Totally new technique I've been wanting to try…*
Timotheus- Teacher, what is the rate of time?

Reesiphinus- First, what are the determinants of rate itself?

T- Something to be measured and units by which to measure.

R- Indeed and In Truth. How to define time?

T- The constriction of infiniteness as an imposition on existence.

R- Inherently and invariably. Within our inflictions, we must attempt to grasp the travel that time has undergone and the quickness with which it did so.

T- How then can we begin our measurements without the ascertainment of either factor? For is not time immobile and its duration unquantifiable?

R- Expertly educed my devoted learner. He enacts the characters of letter and courier equally and immediately, and so far as we can perceive, unceasingly. But as with all irreplicable "normalities" of the universe, we apply our feeble calculations. We use our yardsticks for lifespans and write programs to uncomplicate smiles or tears. These "invariable" elements of the polyentis exist (or rather fasten existence to the others) irrespective of our interference. In fact, we are allowed only inferences.

T- Does not "allow" connote willfulness from a supremacy?

R- Ah, the Truth presents Himself once again. Well done, young one! You have been granted the knowledgement and are correct in that the Most High projects forth as a promontory from the forever flatness of futile humans' understanding. Yet, He wills and wants us to know Him, for what better alternative may we gain from this plane? He excels and exceeds time for He must. We are not dependent on His "I Was." We do not stand idle for His "I Will." We are InFormed with the information that His very name is "I AM." He is the basis of being, the essence of existence, the giver of grandeur... But I digress. For we are to exercise our own salvation with fright and trembling. For it is He who works, actively, presently, in us. Perhaps time is simply a tool he uses for accomplishing His good pleasure. Or, could it not even be the instrument, but a tune, even a note He once played......

(Contemplative pause)

T- Maybe it is a frequency of sequences? Or a sequence of obsequious frequencies? Or is it seemingly -

R- Compose, dear boy. Let us resume our studies on consolidant surrender...

6/1 – 8/10th/2019

MeRe|Y HuM@n

Words are cheap, and these especially are depreciating more quickly.
Archaic ideals say what is wrong in the world comes from "sinning."
This didn't fit my alibi, so my ticked offedness it was brimming.
In my fleeing I found if it's a religion = it can't be "liven."
Yes, I've been there too. And yeah, I hated "truth." I said screw the ichthus, and Baptism has no use. I chucked my Bible across the room, wishing to erase what I knew. Nobody doesn't have tough things that they've been through, but for bitterness or impetus? Each of us has to choose.
Have you had a friend say they'd rather die than regret? Lose sight of lighthouses of hope and miss those decades that they had left? Give a rip and slit the carotid, never get to regret again? Lay down on a heap of towels, fade out, and hope they ascend? Probably even more tragically is when those thoughts occur before 10. I just thank my instigator for showing me what to expect. Not a one of us without Him would have passed on this mental test. Yet the only way to excel is when He extends grace, accept.

Almost had more for that metaphor, for what purpose?
To flex? If that transforms my reason my appealings you should reject. (Sigh) All these topics, byproducts of not being obedient. Makes sense when we only rent – and all we breathe's from his ceiling vents (Ephesians 2:1-2 @ 2). Don't like everyone else? Change YOURself, it is the preempt. We'll only answer for us so just grow and be vehement.
This project's not for us who want our colleagues as our fiends – This is for ladies in radiation leaving clumps of hair in their sinks – This is for young gents who can't find where to stand or what to believe – This is for young women who want to know what they need – This is for the middle men who begin to feel obsolete – This is on behalf of your elders "just listen to us we plea" – Even babies are sapiens, yet more blessed, Ecclesiastes – (1 Cor. 13:13) Scourge us, purge, and pervade the earth with Hope, be replete (Heb. 12:5-11) – By waterway of Faith, flood us with unfathomable Peace (Rom. 5:1 + Phil 4:7) – And greatest of these, teach us Love which will never have kept receipts (1 John 4:9-10).
With these words, I purchase the witness stand, Life is no accident! If it is, then my pretending makes me a Great Mistake applicant. Using every component variation in the alphabet, I still couldn't get your eyesight right like a halibut – sure, you may practice abstinence, obey siete sacraments, but all that can be counterfeit, know before and not after it, the correct path isn't "catholic." For us it's just natural only to see the half of it. Don't be surprised that GOD's the True devil's advocate. Sorry for factuality, the truth always aligns with the Bible.
I wish it wasn't so cause now I know I must shatter my idols.
Hate to love not to be similar, I spin in this sinister cycle.
To rest I'll be laid same as I showed up = <u>person my only Title</u>

Ignore gravestone labels, trust this elementary rhyme.
Better recollected by deeds than monuments when we've died.
When I'm the dessert of worms is when I'm rightly identified.
I'm already a dead man who in Him is made alive.

7/5 – 11/19
I suffer from overexertion
Every portion of me is in hurting
And I feel most purposeful
When I invest into this, my
Written Excursion.

When I get those moments of healing
I'm approached with mistakes wanting repealing
But what's most upsetting is the
Realization that from me there is
No concealing.

Once more, Oh Lord, take the pen again
Distract me if that means I'll be celibate
No need for a return address
Just Stuff and Tuck me into
Your Envelopment

7/13/19
Believe me, you need to breathe, so open up and let it close –
Don't go without O_2, you are not an anaerobe

6/12/19
#Power Up# Hot Now at Krispy Kreme, We thought it would be a nice analogy, I've electrified it, my bright red marquis, everybody's sorry this heart has a vacancy – Apparently, today I've been misbehaving – IDK why, but I'm easily angered – Talked to the Doc, he said that it's a contagion – I must have caught a strain in the midst of my renegading – Triggered my sickness and now my blanco flag's-a-waving – Ocho in my strength alone, time for Faith and Works' consolidation

6/19x2

Despite

In all actuality it's been years of heartbreak, exhaustion, embarrassment, uncomfortability, and pain being general. And then it's not just been my struggle by any means. I have had to be at best a spectator to my family's ongoing turmoil and even my remaining friends' difficulties as they progress. These trials have been triple-faceted as well, aggravating our very hearts by terrorizing our bodies, minds, and souls. Every closest person to me has in some form recently been succumbed to extreme physical malfunction and/or health disruption. In simpler terms, we've all gotten sick; deadly sickly. We have each had to undergo times of varying lengths of emotional distress for widely differing reasonings. Our very mental strongholds have seemingly carelessly been afflicted by foreign ordered ordeals which unfortunately have succeeded in supplanting our optimistic filters with abundances of despair. Past transcendence of the dimensions, our collective spirits appear downtrodden. It's hard to focus on growth when you can't uphold upon. O my soul! These are the precise instants of time when I know I'm exactly where I'm supposed to be located. Of course I realize the anguish it bestows upon myself and my fellow extensions. And I, in addition, apprehensively accept and gracefully welcome tribulations simultaneously. Not the faintest chance will I surpass the passing of the lessons of the tests any time they arrive. But I do know how. I have beheld by His givingness that we are not meant to falter through issues by pushing on and hoping they may be worth a while. We are intended to prosper by way of trials through affirmation and trusting His predesignated process for each individual. The exclusive way to living life to the fullest, is to flourish Despite this life in its fullness.

With Sorrowful mind and Joyfilled heart

-T.R. Edwards

Figure 15. Despite

7/26/19 – 7/31

Verified, I'm anomalous – Nemo deepening in the Nautilus – at the top of the "oddest list" – Popeye with Olive, I've been Sinning Bad but like Paul, not wanting it – A lyrical smitty, yet optimist – A positive consolidant, I've got that neuronal obstinance – You're shocked I got the competence to just go on and on with this...... I'll state the obvious fact that others can say it better, even more can spit swifter, and get their messages quickened with wording more learned and gifted – my pride's eyes see competition, but if you transmit the differences to even one extra witness then I'll sit back and let Any One become headmaster Mathematician – So I'm just sitting digging into my mental filaments – ripping 'em out, pinning 'em down, + getting 'em written Now in this sentence compounded I am dumbfounded at how my wrist is configuring this confounding literacy, but it's just because of assistance I guess I'm more indicative when within photosynthesis – truth is, my skill in fitness is slipping and tho I know some parts of me are against it, there are more parts of a woman I've been missing – and although I am stronger than ever, I'm asking for more forgiveness – That's why I wield this weapen, not to show off to amend – Can't mention who prescribed it, but I'm so thankful for this medicine – If I make it big, those with me now I'll be remembering – If you don't like it, that's fine, I can't find viable reasons for settling – More words = purpose slurred, stumbling back into simple – Mental splurge = edges blur, acting like there is a middle – Fresh at this threshing thing just got handed the sickle – secured the worst of the murders, but was censured and got acquittal – Homeschooled so I'm far more individual – been influenced by the masses since before you could pronounce middle school – I'm just trying to grow in applying wisdom – Objectifying my process + using it for equipping – managing all my tangents, attempting to set up a system – Nobody's worth hearing till someone with insight gives them their <u>listen</u>

SYNCHRONY
Ft. Gracie ^7/15/19 - 22
I miss the fresh
Straight off the lot
Shred off the block
Not a bit overthought
Out Poetry.
Didn't sit and consider
Just let the pen be
A Pillar
Guiding the Israelites
My mind comprised
Of simpler things
Like what to wear
So she'll like me
But not to discard
My humility
Wanting to be this
Older me
But elder me wishes
He were you
Cause now I don't see them as minutes to lose
I see them as artifacts
With innumerable values
I see them as pages
I wish to renew
I see them as raindrops
I want to reuse
Now I'll stop and
Let Grace resume
->

I miss the sweet
Right off the sheet
Cut from the cake
No stress to make
That Poetry
Before society ate it up
I thought that it was tough
But I realized my restrictions
Were someone else's dead ends
Like I was between bookends
But nobody thought to tell me
The when and where
But that was then and there
Now I've freedom in my mind
I and God comprised
Like when I was first alive
No one had infected my thoughts
Perhaps I was my true self
Altered by no one else
Maybe childlike isn't unwise at all
Maybe they just wanted me to feel small
Because the fear of being bigger than them
Was far too much to handle for "the man"
He killed it before it was born
Something so cruel and selfish
Like a handmade dress never worn
They put a chain on my arm
They put a fence in my yard
They put a frame on my art
They put a frame on my art
<-

9/20/19

How outside of the box
Will I travel?
How many levels of my temple will I unravel?
The innate joy from just one personal
Unearthing,
Disrupts the code that worldly life
Invites reverting.
Somewhere behind me, the way turned not to finding
It's only when I close my eyes that
I am walking blindly.
My writing envies when it just wasn't so hurried
Rushing into the next furnace/version is what will burn me
Up surely.

7/23/19 *Insert* Mt. Want

Cause I'm real when it comes to wants
No bread will be leaven you to Wonder then bam!
You'll only relish in fresh French croissants.

Boiled down, it just spoils how we should
Learn 2 respond.

It astounds one, the more they desire, the more they
Tend 2 be gaunt.

Preferably, I pick the bedrock because the base is where
We belong.

Once the climb has begun, it's such a struggle to
Keep from the top.

Every step in which we rise leaves us less satisfied with
What we've got

In this life I fear the zenith, being nothing to do but...

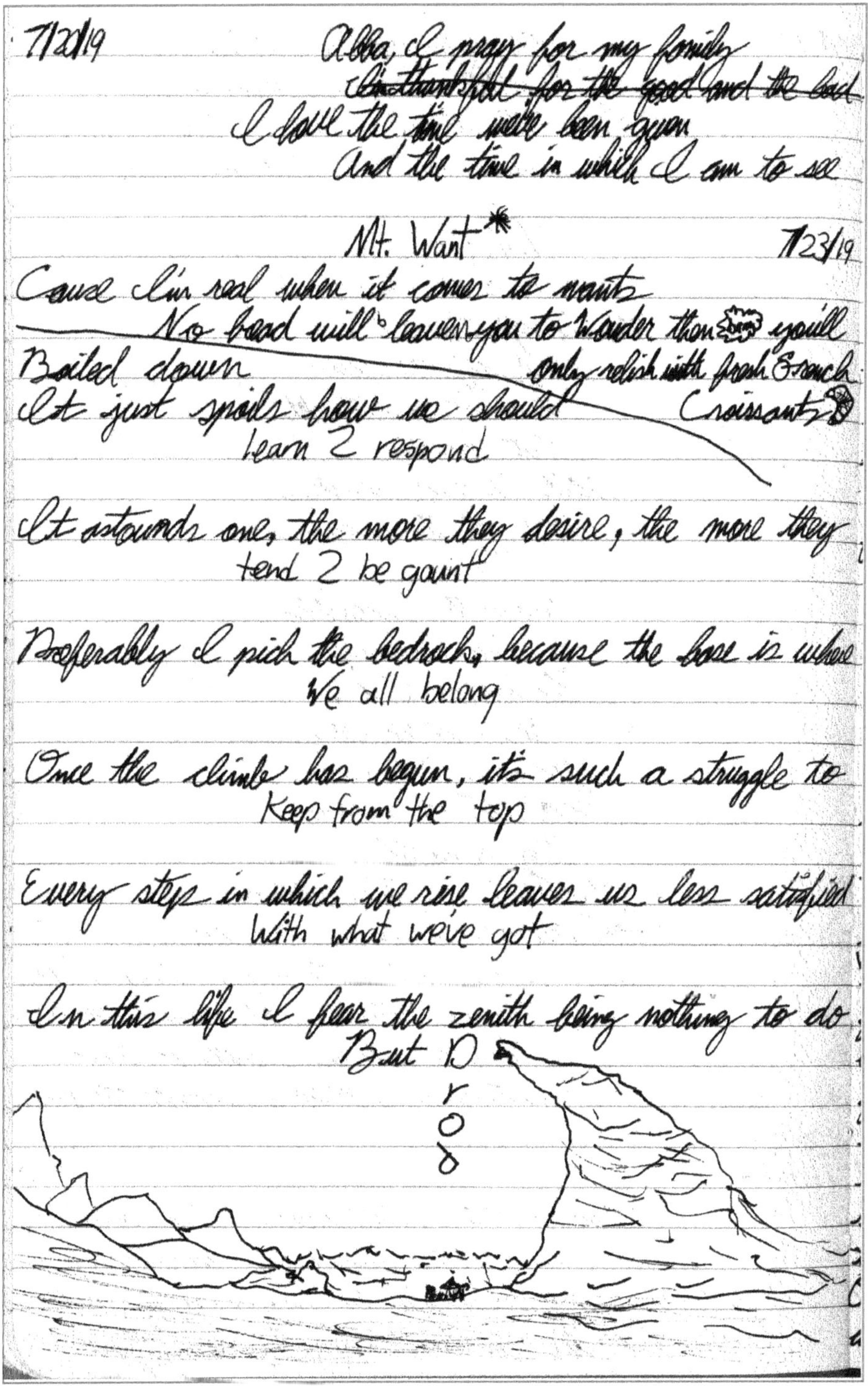

7/20/19

Abba, I pray for my family
~~I'm thankful for the good and the bad~~
I love the time we've been given
And the time in which I am to see

Mt. Want* 7/23/19

Cause I'm real when it comes to wants
No band will leaven you to Wander then you'll
Boiled down only relish with fresh French
It just spoils how we should Croissants
learn 2 respond

It astounds one, the more they desire, the more they
tend 2 be gaunt

Preferably I pick the bedrock, because the base is where
We all belong

Once the climb has begun, it's such a struggle to
Keep from the top

Every step in which we rise leaves us less satisfied
With what we've got

In this life I fear the zenith being nothing to do
But D r o p

Figure 16. Mt. Want

7/28 + 29/19 – I don't know about you, but I'm getting sick of this Timothy – what a carpet bragger acting as if he knows who he's meant to be – Only when he chooses, is he used to coming and to seek – says "He Saves," yet every day he falls to prey to shins glistening – I will not bullsh!t you like this one's intricate, I am just so tired of the changes so I'm aiming to jump the whole gun – maybe found a lady so I'll try to get some = seems like my timeline is taut on months – Pretend to be friends = every woman needs a chum – Balancing on that needle's point of prospective husband and leave him be, shunned – Either way, I guess, I'll get over it – Either way, I don't want to rope her in – I'm only anxious about what I create, and too long I've ruminated, the flood is no longer gated so goodbye to deodorant – Don't even know if I'm wanting what I once had – Don't even care that thick blond hair is a trap – Now I will stomp the rhythm and rhyme and reasoning cause I can't forever write in a rap – Better feel I, I guess, I hope, I think – I don't want regrets more than I want her so at 4 we'll see...... → 7/30/19 – Is it tho? Cause I'm back – I don't think it is cause I haven't done jack – I still wonder if she wanna cause I only saw her hat – asking me for Snapchat getting nervous as a tourist with no landmap – Here's my number girl, hit me up, I'm free, that's a fact – AH! Why's another woman got me so shriekingly distracted? Why'd I realize she's a good person before attractive? Why can I pen it like Rembrandt but never can get it adlib? Maybe I'll find who matters when my matters are not a habit.

End Tim

8/2/19

PHANTOM PAINS

it's the best way to explain
what she did to me
held my favorite appendage
then when I least expected it
she ripped it off and pinned it to the wall
now me and my love are separate
these days I'm dragging my jagged limb
or what's left of it
sitting here wishing that I had already bled to death
and every time I exercise my affection
the peg in it
settles in better, so I'm just saying the hell with it

8/2/19 PHANTOM PAINS

It's the best way to explain
What she did to me
Held my favorite appendage
Then when I least expected it
She ripped off and pinned it to the wall
Now me and my love are separate
These days I'm dragging my jagged limb
Or what's left of it
Sitting here wishing that I had already bled to death
And every time I exercise my affection
The peg in it
Settles in better so I'm just saying the hell with this

At the most difficult place I've been in life
I need people with me to help decide
but She closed the door to those with the best advice
10/1/19 This love with me will forever cry

Figure 17. Phantom pains

8/4/19

I do fall, occasionally Bale and strike my face like Duvall. Why? Asked Mr. Wayne. To rebel as Richard Nugent or Pulitzer in the musical, never been good with names of movies… that's it! The Newsies. 1 A.M. and I'm confusing, mentally constipated. This Day's Green and tonight this Insomniac's writing's Dookie… OK, Nimrod, let's try again. Such a tight rein on my bridle it's equestrian. Cannot canter in triplets, Benedicts, Secretariat, riposte and parry it, bearing flintlock and scabbard, my savior gave me His rapier; it was cutless until I carried it. Yo, let me help with that, you need to sheathe mental trash. Here's a twelve pack of Hefty bags, a katana, and a Kendo mask. Alfred Lord Tennyson, Edison, and Mrs. Evelyn better never be rendered negligent. If their efforts were able to be injected, I'd carry them like an epi-pen. Let them enter my head through the brain stem, use it as a "take when necessary" type of medicine. I'm flying free of the harlot's den, on the outskirts of Charlotte's Webb. Bourne with preceding David well-called in brawls as Jason and hunting down Ryan for saving. So many tricks with Mr. Damon… My IRAhab is worth acclaiming.

8/9/19

I realized I really began writing as a fluke; as a dare to myself. Then I was infatuated at the first drawn blood of my pen. I could cohere my rabid thoughts on the calmly awaiting page. Mostly, I've written personal experiences or aspirations, but it's been gr8 to see my own writing evolve, adapt, and hopefully mature. Sometimes, I make things so simple probably anyone could get it. Other times I hide meanings so deep in lyrical pyramids it's a miracle if I can remember even near to the instance. God really, truly, simply gave me writing for the last sentence's reasoning: to think and have this "outlet" to plug into to use as an "inlet" to help my everyday life. It all started out so simple, and I can't wait to see where it will flow next.

9/10/19

Did you miss me? Did you miss me? ¿ǝɯ ssıɯ noʎ pıᗡ
Cause I've been missing. I been giving my best to this "fit in" thing, but I just can't keep up with it, it's clipping my wings. I want to make taking breaks history. I thought a little R+R would revitalize me. Yet I guess I checked off the wrong list in itemizing. Exhibited what it is I'll do when the realization of relativism begins cherry picking my cynicism. I think I'm addicted to the intuitiveness which issues initiative individualism. Socratic mediocrities offer wobbly morality, got awful commonalities never trust that rationality. Presently I am entering into empathy where every separate section has validity worth remembering.

9/18/19

I suppose the allurement of self-control and self-efficiency is not tempting enough for some.

9/20/19 for 9/11/19

3 years. I haven't done much for that long consistently in my life. A message to future self = Don't ever EVER forget who gave you this {HIM} and just grow in gratefulness. Lately, I've been almost overwhelmed with all the writing projects, and I thought that taking a break would help me clarify. Another message to future self = It doesn't. The thought processes just get more confusing, and life gets construed. However, as I'm coming back to my life support,

I am ready to take more massive steps towards an unknown yet certain future. At the moment I'm trying to balance out development of my mind, body, and soul so that it's simultaneous. I also am finding my true passion is not writing to demonstrate it, but to just grow myself closer to the mold God sculpted for me.

9/27/19

I can't expect them to think
When they don't eat
I can't expect them to see
When they don't seek
I can't expect them to reap
When they don't feed
I can't expect them 2 B
When they don't need

Let me abhor what you do Lord. Desiring affection, but not yours. Letting my thoughts drift to shifty side streets. Wishing to be alone but wanting to still be seen. Sometimes I even think that I've beaten pride, but all my writings begin and end with "I"! You're overthinking! Forget the rhyme and meter and hone in on rhythm and reason. When I'm happiest I feel lost. It's so healing unveiling scars. As the tree wings decay my best memories come to flaunt. While the list keeps getting shorter, I need these people even more. Talk about a release date but things change, I can't be sure. How many decisions did I enact to appease somebody's ego? Nobody who really knows me will be tearful when my chariot swings low. I bet God to test me, as of right now, He's 3/0. When you look back at your progress you aren't watching where your feet go. *Break up that Quartet, and saying it plain for a sec.* A "Professional Complainer" is not what I will be labeled as. I stick to a "General Premise" I know He's placed before me, and We fight off the spirit of fear which swirls with more fervor when I'm nearing the presence of the purported Prince of Power and Peace. It sounds so simple, but this is a hint of my current issues. Just Run with the Son to the Father by my Plus One ;)

10/4/19
Only my best performance, so holding out for those goosebumps
Tho somehow the best ones show up slowly from dumb luck
Ckc ckc, c'mon buddy, it's that time to upset the tempo, get open like when Renfrow's headed to the Dead zone
Our only defenses against mental sepsis is getting relentless for correctness = why can't it be simple like Jethro?
I have such an existential MO
I cannot quit growing so I empty out my friend zone
Got the funk of a Republican
The protruding tongue and stuck-up thumbs for everyone's suffrage
Won't lie, I was getting redundant and to me self-ineffectiveness is repugnant
Thus, my flying free like a phoenix from structure as a rebuttal to Umbridge
Please trust this
When anyone says they can treat you right
They only see enough of you for them to have a good time
Usually a few nights
But if we want the long-term satisfaction, we'll choose life
And besides, what's more short-lived than a modern kid's rise?
Silence is getting me heated
My writing's so not cohesive
If I got a genie, each of my three would be times with people to relive
God is such a vortex
I and my 3 keep exploring
Never boring

And never finely, my life is filed down coarsely
But now all I see is His blessing when lessons I've been absorbing
Toning down my diet
(something to do with food) yada yada... how I eye it
Dude, I don't know when this book is coming out
I definitely am afraid and it's naïve to think those fears will check out once it is released
Because when it is received It's Most Important that everyone feels Him and worships Him beside me
Next up come the naysayers, the "educators," today's kids label them haters, they who from day one
Won't let go of this world so they hang on
But I've got omnipatience, so I appreciate it
Can I uphold my position against the increased attrition?
With opinions come opposition, I see them, I'm an optician
So with this infinite vision, I'm just on a quick mission
Questioning and double-checking, constant, personal inquisition
Or am I just chasing a feeling?
Do I actually know my meaning?
Because it's shocking that acceptance brings no happiness
Yet it may be the groundwork of all my endeavors
What really tickles my fancy is furthering my concurrence
The heat with me has always worked adversely
So I am over thrilled when I feel Autumn a'churning
What do you like more, ME, thinking oddly or godly?
Got a big case of heartbreak + wherever I am I carry it
No need to call in 808 = no prosperity or visionary yet
Only so far as God's in the right perspective
Can me and my buddy's imaginings and realities be connəcted
Going it on alone keeps me sleeping wretched
Yet falling asleep on my desk writing lets me awake feeling blessed
It's really this simple: I was turning into a villain
Every choice I would not make, I was getting more willing
Now I'm THE best evidence for the freedom from Jesus' recompense

Trust me, I want justice for Hypatia, so I like #5 addressed to
Galatia = For freedom Christ has set us free
One touch, now I bum rush desperately

Figure 18. Root of the fruit

10/7/19

Recondite = Pertaining to or dealing with very profound, difficult, or abstruse subject matter\ known or understood by relatively few, esoteric, arcane, obscure

10/7/19

4 years, here's some more tears. Dad's sadness still gives me fear.
All I wonder is how proud would you be Mamaw?
Cause I could use your brutal honesty more often than not.
I look back and love every minute we shared, from you going down
That slide
To our infamous Gatlinburg drive!
Fried bologna sandwiches and Richie Rich
To your soft clothes and all the jokes at Christmas.
I can't wait to see your updated body.
I promise we'll go waltzing and
How terrific to skip with you with no coughing!
My level of love and admiration for you is off the charts,
And I can only awe at the thought of you rearing up those 3,
We're applauding!
Pretty much I am thrilled picturing sharing another hug to
remember. This family's indebted to your love and spunk
keeping us together.
Thank you for all you gave me that I know of
And for all the hidden things I'll see when it's my
turn to head up,
See you soon!

October 13th, 2019 on Hebrews 3

"[12]Take care, brothers, lest there be in any of you an evil, unbelieving heart, leading you to fall away from the living God. [13]But exhort one another every day, as long as it is called 'today,' that none of you may be hardened by the deceitfulness of sin. [14]For we have come to share in Christ, if indeed we hold our original confidence firm to the end."

Lord, I pray now that you would engrave these parts of your truth onto my heart, that I would live as such without even focusing on it. I crave your true fellowship today. I want to stay awake, God, and grow in the practicality of Your Word. My writings are yours Lord, and I just want to know that you're guiding me and blessing my entire process. Please protect and bless my family and few friendships and mature each of us so that we may push each other constantly towards you.

10/9/19

The war we declared at 3 rages on and one more battle was waged yesterday, yip. I almost masturbated. Thankful I overcame, but still hate I entertained it. Yes, I know that Jesus saves, but God's also got a gavel and I'm afraid to disobey Him. Only the 3rd party can warn me where on the scale that I'm behaving. Now I'm aggravated; distracted from my vast amount of massive past failures. My growth was so apparent, that's why a low blow such as that might just have been the final nail to seal what I'm encased in. From the inside, I'll set this box a'blazing, watching the flames so calmly, I am waiting. So thrilled to see the devil's face he makes when I will break it. I'm writing this to know that history is what place this is taking. By no ounce of my strength, so I praise Him! I am amazed and enraged at you Satan. But now we've tasted your blood and we'll chase it.

I think I'll miss you when you're baking.

"Brisk Weather Inspires." – Mr. Charlie

10/11/19

Autumn is brewing
The daybreak is cooling
As my peers start to complain of the frost
My head gears begin moving

The wind's been cooing
Less clouds allow the sky's bluing
Somehow the cold's a catalyst for my heart
And it's so soothing

Styles are improving
Girls are not as nuding
All the ones you would not want went indoors
Not in the mood for wooing

All these –'s I'm shooing
Word, this excerpt is goofy
This'll be in the bonus features:
Deleted scenes from the movie

10/13/19

Who's bringing sexy back?
Our definition is so out of whack
We know the smart ones are not buying that
Like when you get one nicknamed "Alley cat"

Figure 19. Film — Fine

Rolling!
10/14/19
Here's one of my peeves' pettings – Life is incredibly messy – It set the trend of bad settings – When we look back it had crappy editing – Cast and crew mos def not worth mentioning – Hopefully maxed out the budget lent – Yet never ready to get to the expected ending – Don't wait up for after credits scenes – How's the audience feel about that legacy? – Are you bereft of everything but empathy – Or lesser, left rendered envying? – Every millisecond we're effecting – Enemy or Effendi? – Both of those questions best meant for remembering – Just entertaining? Semi-underrated? Or mostly grossly underestimated – Notice the skipping over of Emmy nominated – No way it can be overstated = the overpaid will always say what greater hate should be related – But it's empty – The best method for a life well spent is to blend in medley – Investing in everyone never gets us to the end and guessing – So before we're set in the collection let's ponder the messages we're sending – To who's next, to better our best and emulate it – Then at peace we may rest atop the shelving – So He **II** invented death as the edge of a DVD, intended to be an entrance to eternal infinity. Empowering to be a cinematographic masterpiece. Ask "what a lovely fact, for me to get my own entry" ------- Finè

Y/E/S
I'm on a quest, it's
To where my desk is
No view in front of me, I don't know where I'm headed
I got a wall ahead of me, so we keep it reflective
Whenever I see them
I'm eager to treat them as even
Like Wii and then DS
Nintendo's a weakness
The remote's wrestling my pen for attention
Yet here again to emend
And leering at my dear friend

He's jeering and my ear's red
But I enjoy an upset
I'm Emerson = I transcend.
I infringe my limits
To rescind my sinning
Don't care if I'm winning
Because I ignore echelons
A self-taught eschatologist, joy junkie, and a celibate
Who gets the biggest kick from time spent with his relatives
What the world tells him is the best sh!t,
He's skeptical and not with a mile-long pencil does he mess with
Always hoping to be alone, yet his love for others is endless
God, when I was 7 and restless, crying in bed, yes, He had read this
The Testament says He's relentlessly jealous, now I'm defended
Left breathless with nothing else but a blessed life with an unlimited line of credit
Free of debt and complete freedom on how to spend it.
Now we set up a checklist.
Let's fill it up with X's

10/16/19
I believe even Eve would leave me in the Garden of Eden. The only one who had True Love was spiritually conceived. If you're reading this, do me a favour: go to the next page, this one for me is needed. Personally knew you a couple months. But from the few times we talked, I could tell you were a special one, and your eyes kept my mind occupied. The pieces fell and connected, and I loved to watch. You were so cute when we communicated in the hall. Once we'd agreed, I approached your dad to inquire as to what he thought. I need that courage again from when I met him and your mom. Never held my head up higher since when their respect I'd bought. I see kids my age now playing "do you like me if..." and think knock it off. Me and you didn't give 2, we had all callers blocked. As we chased love it got rough, show me any that are not. If I had to pick it, the best visit was when I came in March. You know I could go on and on, the rhyme would run out first. I wish it were simple to have you back like using every single

word......... But who knows, maybe God meant for me to have nothing lifelong. Cause then in one unexpected wreck, I lost my only earned Heart

Of course it's relatable, it's truth

October 17th, 2019
C'mon babe, let's run away to Brisbane. Let your hair hang and your hips lay, next to me as we observe the waves. As they lap and as each one crashes that much more would you love me back. We'd steal away to California, but why stop there cause I wouldn't dare to bore ya. In a perfect world, we could board a ship heading the long way to Florida. We could tour and name each island on the way to the Orient, but we'd have to stay a few nights on the shoreline of Corsica. There's no one with whom I'd rather explore Europe, for the sole feeling of being so historical. End in Iceland, make you my wife and......... then on to New York! No need for a realtor, financier, and all, we'd travel and love for a living, our house would be the world. North America'd be our backyard. North Africa, our sandbox, Asia: a winter getaway, from Antarctica, watch the stars. Aurora Australis point us to the Pacific to cool us off. And if we wanted some alone time, our night satellite for some R+R. While we could rear the kids, I'd build something to actually travel far. Milky Way rounds for a Greyhound, pardon me Elon and screw Mars. Andromedae and galaxies await, say hey to Vega when we depart. We'd definitely eat popcorn seeing cluster scenes against the backdrop of dark. I didn't think I'd get so into this when I began to start. These markings of ink can't be purchased at a local mart. I'm dragging this happiness out cause in the morning it will be marred. Can't break up the rhyme now, here comes the final part: there's myriads, but the main reasons I need this are

10/21st/19 – Psalm 4:2+3
"O men, how long shall my honor be turned into shame?
How long will you love vain words and seek after lies?
But know that the Lord has set apart the godly for himself; the LORD hears when I call to him."

10/22/19

Writer's Block

Truly, truly, I can promise you I've never had it. Only paused to contemplate on which concept for grabbing. At least, that's how I picture it. Cause babe, I've never had a blank space, hey Taylor Swift, my sister's been your biggest listener since Picture to Burn, but she couldn't demonstrate it because so many little girls' parents were so much richer than hers. But never in her wildest dreams did her teardrops fall on guitar strings. Now I see what I mean, I could always be writing ethereal material pen-in-hand when dying. But words are only worth typing if I trust God. Cause I won't be out of the woods until He performs my Dust-off. Best to let my tongue stop, then my head gets unclogged, welcome heaven, no Sonblock, me and my pen pal prepared at all times = mental gun cocked. So when I hear some peoples' writings are like stuck rocks, I pity them cause I only see alphabetical blocks. We just be spending our free time rearranging them. Stacking them so that we can see another angle and, returning with good news from the master as their chamberlain. Man oh man I cannot say that I'm caught, up because my time here is lifelong, unsusceptible to the pain threw away Tylenol. Trinity of trinities, we live in 3's, even tripodal. When I quit writing I begin to die from my withdrawals. But it's a healthy addiction, thus I will never cycle off.

10/25/19

Good On Demand

Guys, lemme handle this. We all agree we have the right to free rambling, and we can amble on scamming 'em all trampling all over this wonderful life we've been handed, so I handed mine to Him and He in no way hampers it. Life in fullness, it's glamorous and imagine that we're just skimming it. He's my advantage and Santa's bag can't manage a candle to Him and this gift. Cause my CEO quit the business of limits to manufacture each individual to His image. Tho, dimly we see through the window, all of us must confront we're sick with a syndrome and that's why it's dumb to be shaken up by symptoms. Sick of being human? Here's the cure to your condition and you're so close! Like glucose and fructose, and the best I'll ever do is hand out anecdotes, hoping I'm salt in their mouths and lampposts along their roads.

Figure 20. Know

10/26/19
Me and dad in the past were watching the tube's eye On a documentary about businessmen in the woods, mind you, in the South Appalachians, the mountains, yes, that's the blue kind. With their stills and their no teeth and they're hilarious manufacturing moonshine.
I laughed, then my dad clapped me on the back and said "that's your bloodline." My jokes croaked "Unlike Otis, they didn't all have to do time." So as I eat crow, I see now why that side of my family's so uptight. Alcohol brought so many Southern families to rubble. It befuddles me, what's its use again? Because my memory's muddled. Took a few generations to sober up, but it's still here real subtle. And each of us has slipped and sipped, so we're always being humble. The sooner that we nip the bud the quicker we won't stumble. And a better off world we'll leave so our kids will have different struggles.

10/28/19 1 Corinthians 3 is an awesome explanation of needing God as our foundation and not being "mere men."

11/3/19
Take my eyes off of Him get to judging. I make God strike out then the right route gets fuzzy. Yet He lets only me budge me, a chess player in a brutal game of rugby. I have to find God's Grace in my life to put Him in the right Place in my life. I was tripping on "what did" and "what will" that I'd quit living with thanks in my stride. I acted out the falsehood believing I became Christ, so focused on rescuing truth I forgot to save mine. Put limits on influence; best advice I got was from God at a gravesite. He told me how it grows old when I romanticize it. He asked me to enjoy this gift and forget fantasizing. View this truth through manic eyes, and He only wants us to want His sanitizing.

10/31/19 – 2/4/20 $$$$$$$$$$$$$$$$$$$$$$$$$$$$$$$$$$

Let’s mention our money culture.
I know some things that nobody’s probably told ya.
What if I said that We’re the ones getting sold bruh.
And we should really get less the more that we grow up.
Governmental skeletal fractals handle all our financials.
When it gets equivocal, they go invisible like Randall.
Consumerism chews your inner mind, come have a sample.
We’ll stalk up on the market, hearts becoming mansion shambles.
Hunting bands of Grants and Franklins will make you deranged and.
We think we’ll be sanguine while we are chasing anguish.
Only your soul is sacred so quit complaining.
Cause the things that we can’t buy are the things that are worth saving.
And it seems that we gain everything when we begin proclaiming.
Our retributive bankruptcy.
Cause once hemoglobin’s stagnant, we’re way past A1C.
Encase the point was missed, focus on latency.
Don’t get caught in that dog crap called Bureaucracy.
There’s no need to issue an apology.
Cause we’re sorry for the folly in their policies.
But the farthest they regard are our commodities.
We think we’re deferring detriment.
If we can earn them Benjamins.
When did currency purchase any sentiment?
Or accrue any mental regimen?
Flush your money down the pot and I believe you’ll be amazed.
Plug your stomach’s tongue and give food to bums for a day.
Join with me in poignancy and our joy will be saved.
Cause denarii can’t buy happiness.
They only buy distractions.
And the only real estate you own’s
The one you put your casket in.

-<{$♥$}>-

11/8/19
Mr. Heath and I asked for God's eyes
And He gave them.
But lately I've been pretending they're mine
And haven't thanked Him.
Instead of viewing people with hope, I used them as if
They were a scope and at everyone I've been aiming.

It makes it hard because I see
Everyone's potential.
It almost seems like I can sense
Their power levels.
This is why it's killing me to watch people so willingly
Not fight the current but settle.

I never thought that God giving me insight
Would make it difficult.
Even those who don't know me know the truth
It's pitiful.
Complaining about the weight I place on myself
But there's less pressure at the center so it's spelled
centrifugal.

So in this quest you just purchased
Equity.
The only thing I've learned is that
I haven't especially.
Our life is wreckage if we mess with it carelessly,
So I'd just love for you to invest in this trek with me.

First Project of 2020 =

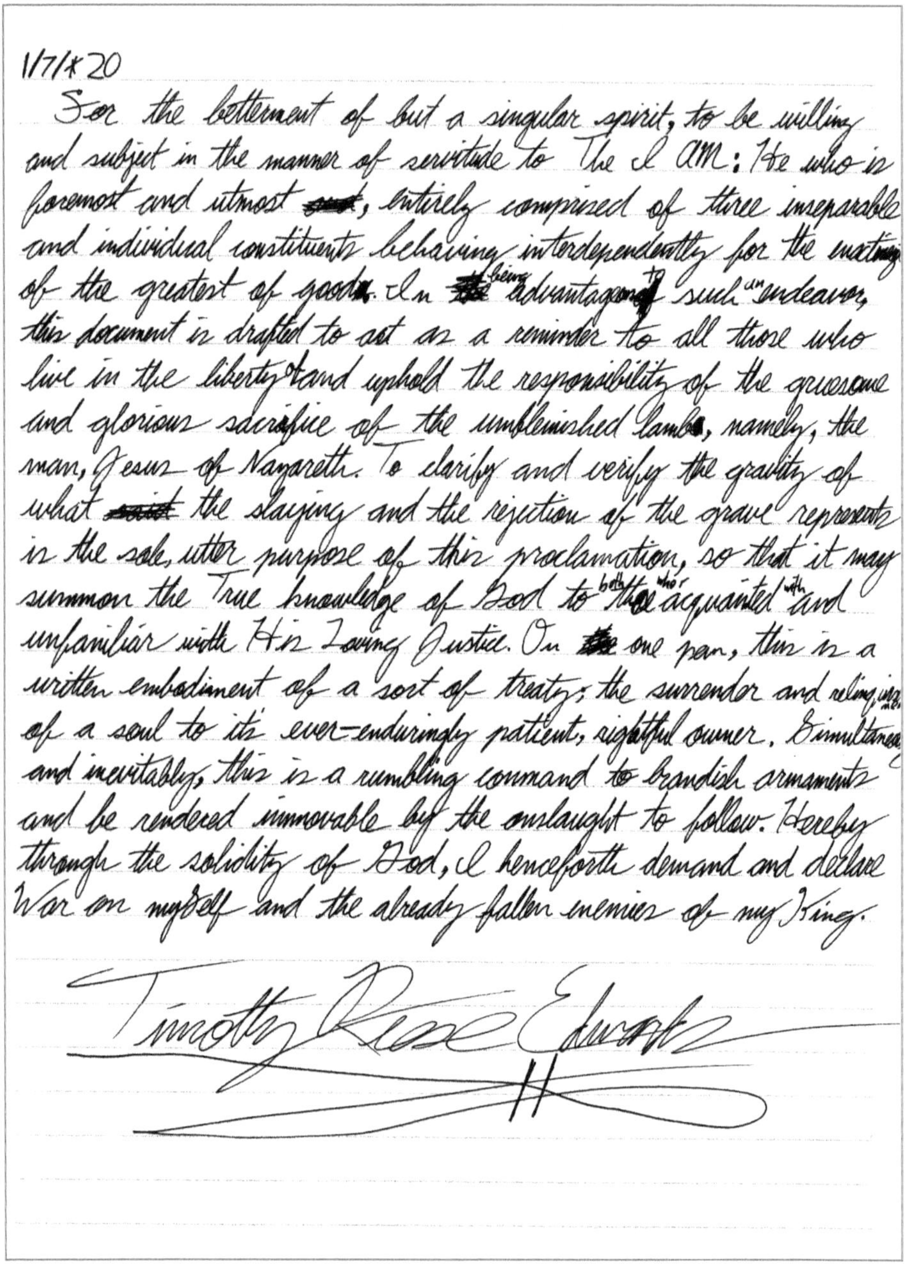

1/7/*20

For the betterment of but a singular spirit, to be willing and subject in the manner of servitude to The I AM: He who is foremost and utmost, entirely comprised of three inseparable and individual constituents behaving interdependently for the making of the greatest of goods. In being advantageous to such an endeavor, this document is drafted to act as a reminder to all those who live in the liberty and uphold the responsibility of the gruesome and glorious sacrifice of the unblemished lamb, namely, the man, Jesus of Nazareth. To clarify and verify the gravity of what the slaying and the rejection of the grave represents is the sole, utter purpose of this proclamation, so that it may summon the True knowledge of God to both those acquainted with and unfamiliar with His Loving Justice. On one paw, this is a written embodiment of a sort of treaty: the surrender and relinquishment of a soul to it's ever-enduringly patient, rightful owner. Simultaneously and inevitably, this is a rumbling command to brandish armaments and be rendered immovable by the onslaught to follow. Hereby through the solidity of God, I henceforth demand and declare War on myself and the already fallen enemies of my King.

Timothy Reese Edwards II

Figure 21. Declaration of war

11/12/19
Entering an extra level of discretion, cause I'm too mature to call it depression. But I'm not really sad, in fact I welcome it. I know it's better to be upset than be pretending it; had never happened, I acted as if I'd attained some famed position. I hadn't thought of solemnity as a requisition. It's weird to hydrate hoping to get yourself to cry. Man overboard! I jumped ship = the ark of the covenant made with my eyes. Birthday wants are just wishes to go back in time. Sure it seemed hard, but I see now it was perfectly fine. I can't just hold on to fond memories, so I made mental shrines. And when I'm not worshipping the one true God I stop on by. That's when I can empathize with those two guys at Columbine. Late hours without her are our flower children zombified – 12/2/19 – I don't know what has caused me not to write

But I can tell myself one thing = step off the Oxygen pipe

11/13/19
Isaiah 52:7 "How beautiful upon the mountains are the feet of him who brings good news, who publishes peace, who brings good news of happiness, who publishes salvation, who says to Zion, 'Your God Reigns'."

12/22/19
Fear of potential.
Fear of success.
Vomit in attention.
Sorry for the mess.
People asking questions. Can't prepare for this. Screw spontaneous, get a fat F on their quiz. Who I want to be is hiding in this pen. From my chicken scratches to my living habits, yeah, what's the disconnect? I want to be the person that I think you think I am. Obedient Me's calling me and he's clapping his hands. The only thing impeding me is feeling like a lamb. So you doubtful, prideful man: I command you to be ($*)#*$.

1/08/20 – 1/18/20
Cold fingers by the creek and feeling expedient – I feel pretty dead but being obedient – I don’t like my own way, think it’s convenient – You, reading, critiquing my rhythm switch like “I’m not seeing it” -—- Struggle through the stress of this muddled mess. Oh, here we go again, all the questioning. Like when all this ends, will I be content? Cemented in that sentence is unlimited contention. Cause everywhere I’ve been wants to retort with a negative. It makes me squirm; will I ever discern between who my friend and Grendel is? And I go alone on the lonesome road Solitary Street, and all I have to eat is my belly meat and a can of beats. And I can’t see as long as I panic myself to sleep in a world full of mannequins that are too manic to blink. Very few of them will just man up and peak into the expanse spanning cause it’s too good to be free, and it hurts my pride to believe that even the worst of all mankind has as much right as me to bow before the Holy Uno and join the family.

S
H
E
E
E
E
E
S
H

Boy, oh boy, here’s another useless ramble. I just massaged a swab up my butt, and here’s the sample. Any time you read what I write it’ll be a gamble. I like to think that I make us weep, on the next page, make a heart bleed, turn over again and laugh till we have to pee, and finally on the 4 count, force our meanings to rethink. I want to have you sweat, cringe, and think "this is so me" – If only. Cause if you actually want to know God, you've got to show me. And if you're the hero at the end of the story, then blow me. I am and meet people like that every day and they're what I don't need.

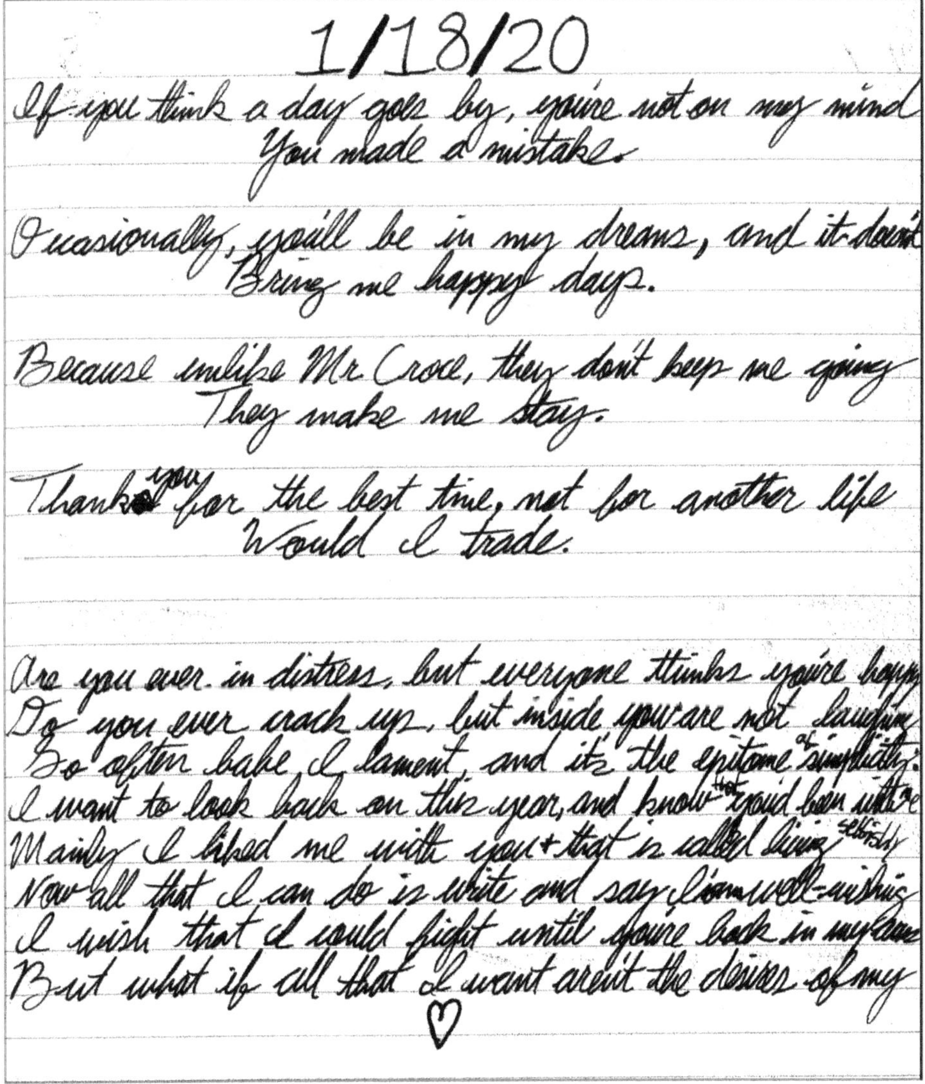

1/18/20

If you think a day goes by, you're not on my mind
You made a mistake.

Occasionally, you'll be in my dreams, and it doesn't
Bring me happy days.

Because unlike Mr Croce, they don't keep me going
They make me stay.

Thank you for the best time, not for another life
Would I trade.

Are you ever in distress, but everyone thinks you're happy
Do you ever crack up, but inside you are not laughing
So often babe I lament, and it's the epitome of simplicity.
I want to look back on this year, and know that you'd been with me
Mainly I liked me with you + that is called living selfishly
Now all that I can do is write and say I'm well-wishing
I wish that I could fight until you're back in my days
But what if all that I want aren't the desires of my ♥

Figure 22. 1.18.20

1/18/20

If you think a day goes by, you're not on my mind
You made a mistake.

Occasionally, you'll be in my dreams, and it doesn't
Bring me happy days.

Because unlike Mr. Croce, they don't keep me going
They make me stay.

Thank you for the best time, not for another life
Would I trade.

Are you ever in distress, but everyone thinks you're happy?
Do you ever crack up, but inside you are not laughing?
So often babe I lament, and it's the epitome of simplicity
I want to look back on this year, and know that you'd been with me
Mainly I like me with you and that is called living selfishly
Now all that I can do is write and say I am well-wishing
I wish that I could fight until you're back in my arms
But what if all that I want aren't the desires of my
♥

Why unto me this gift ------ This hit
Did cosmos bestow with
1/21/20 Her blind, wild heave?
Or conquest pass down in his rowdy crowd tease?
Perhaps
Morosity tossed me into the aristocracy?
Or the cows' bells clanged Home on the Range?
Presumably only one
Or nil
Or
Maybe all of these
I find that one can rhyme all of the time, but just symbolically
'Tis stressing and discouraging to vault out of the boxing ring

But this gun and ink are
My pogo springs
And I pose my inquiry once again.
Did the gears just fit or the shoes just fill
With my meager contribution?
Or did the grand old poet's joy hurl over the cliff's brim?
Still I wayfare
Why into me this pit ---– This bliss

1/24/20
Don't get you wrong, you always miss certain people.
But there are advantageous quirks for being single.
Freedom to dream of threading the needle through the peephole.
Speaking in tongues like a Pentecostal keynote.
Got one squawking and squealing like a seagull.
All positional permutations and ending in the fetal.
Now those are analogies you can't even find at Lidl.
I'm still on the straight and narrow-minded like ole Cecil. That's why I think He still smiles on me kneeling near the steeple. But I tell me what, this old flesh is so feeble.

1/27/20 – 2/11/20
Sometimes, my blood pumper jumps a thump
Like when one of the right types reaches out
Whacking me with her eyesight
Occasionally, my blood pumper jumps a thump
Like when I realize the stupendousness of
God letting me live twice
At times, my blood pumper jumps a thump
Like when I run from my head to
Truly feel alive
Sporadically, my blood pumper jumps a thump
Like as fear upsets my depths of
Peace, potential begins to arise

Uncontrollably, my blood pumper jumps a thump
Like when temptations' falsities fall on me
Engaging my thighs
Erratically, my blood pumper jumps a thump
Like in inexplicable calm of heart with
A body fraught with fright

1/28/20
"If in Christ we have hope in this life only, we are of all people most to be pitied." – 1 Corinthians 15:19

2/6/20
People don't care where you've been – They care about the circumstance and what you did – Cause they want some of your success themselves – When they can't understand the fight starts after the final bell – Place me in a closet cause I don't want a sarcophagus – Just imagine how different it'd be if a genius killed Romulus – Maybe, just maybe, one day we'll end up making a song of this - I don't want my reward in full so I'm trying to fill the offering. On God's tour, He's showing me so many things needing clobbering. Everybody talks babe, thinking they know, it's cacophonous. Those amidst the first fruits admit we don't, so we open our Zondervans.

2/11/20 *to Know Your Enemy 1/2/3...*
I want God on telepathy
Broadcasting mentally
My life interconnectedly ryy y y y y
Trying to write respectively
What's death + heavenly
While on spiritual ecstasy ~~~
Preparing for the revelry
Sharing eclectically
From Beaufort to Beverly ^'^*^

2/18/20 – I know I'll always be my biggest fan because when I write I know God's pen-in-hand

2/13/20
We're young and impressionable... so be impressed
Don't let someone's surmizations determine your success
Cause nothing ever looks as good when it's been undressed
While carrying the banner of progress
Everyone's corrupt and suppressed
So hail the bearers of personal unrest
I be calling me an anti-rebel – "Follow directions, wear eye protection, and always remember to settle" – Curse a name, bless the face, and good kids never meddle – There will be a darker spot in which to nestle – The key factor in rebellion is it's ever-developing – I've been trying to make a mental system to spite religion – But schematics get problematic when they're not simple as if 4 children – so today I really hate my guts and I'm trying to spill them – Launching attacks, staunchly attached and some are even hidden – When I hold glow I must go home not the one with my family – The old folks with their no hopes feels like cracking my face with a dobro. Youth lies saying life's flowing so slow, but it doesn't, catch it in a rear-naked choke hold. Death is all that can showboat, and I wish the departed had GoPros. But one thing's for certain: it's YODO. Let's punch and crunch our way to the soul's yolk, where equality's awful = we're all broke. But if we make His blood puddles our abode, our vessels sink as our new spirits float – So let's give this Matrix a reload – cause once we understand the real fight, we'll be like Neo – We may not be driving, but that won't stop a repo – We may not be fighting back, but that don't mean that he won't

2/19/20
I'd rather be disconsolate
Than
Argue in the kid's ball pit

2/27/20

Everybody turning out to be a righteous judge –
I just find it funny cause now there are none to trust –
Everyone of us is mighty till it's time to be tough – We're
all creative geniuses until it has to be off the cuff – I must
unsweep these things about me from underneath the rug – I
think so much about myself, I'm no diamond in the rough – I'll
only act as if I'm Aladdin if I'm zapped by your love – And I'll
only be the recipient if I bathe in His blood

2/28/20

My LORD, My GOD
Deliverer of my Soul
You're My first responder
And My final resting place
May you be the limelight of this life
And may your joy be my delight
What am I without You?
But a pretentious liar hiding that I'm lost
In you I'm found, where self is no more
Apart from the portions of me You restored.

3/2/20 – 3/3/20

Narcissisickness
I can only really be myself when it's just myself around
Paranoia's my annoyance if I can't dumbfound
This healthful vessel runs amuck but never runs aground

To be one's own hero appears to produce synergy
To live in the prison within begins to seem like liberty
But I long-since slit my inner peace = to purpose I'm reverting

There's no room for failure when I'm playing by my rules
Impossible standards be lifeless, and I challenge to a duel
My life for my sake's ending, and I'm unraveling the spool

Figure 23. Hartbreak

There's always something to break your heart, but will you help it?

3/10/20

I'm here and I'm nearing some ends, and my mind trembles and fidgets and spins. I'm scared to rebegin and fear being here again; it's like a great, rank woolly mammoth of the brain. I'm forcing myself to let go of what I won't. I'm coercing me to know that I don't. Oh, there I go, here's the show, lights grow low, I liked when my eye and cheek bones were bruised. Cause when we're in pain you're not so confused. Not obeying's still behaving, I blame Mr. Hughes. I don't want to placate or vacate in this era. Because "to be Abram I must need a Sarai." I'm at war with myself and the skirmish just may scare ya. But I drove off my motives into the cove of being open, and I'll surf the incoming waves of the Come-Being ocean. It just stinks cause authenticity means I need to be Broken.........

3/13/20

WEST-WARD

Our plane skates the space up above, the earth's sky froth like a blanket of vaporous lint tufts. 34 Fahrenheit is what the pilot recorded. My body's not prepared, but my brain is all for it. Change of pace and scenery will hopefully reinstigate me to do what I love and love who He is, to be grateful still more as He gracefully gives.

7/14/20 – On "Spring Trip" — My worries hitched a ride with the flurries, and they scurry away. I ponder what man is = as I encounter the sky's dandruff. Cozy there on the knoll of snow-topped stones. Not so far off from the chopped log trove.

3/21/20

Arrogance is ignorance and ignorance is bliss

Your big head fits nice on that neck till it's given a twist

April 16 2Knock2On Asphalt
All it took was some facial/dental trauma to knock my effective mental on again. A large sigh and a laugh from seeing the sonagram. I was acting like the mentally retarded llama. I was lucky, I only kn#cked my front teeth, and did no damage to my medulla oblongata. Before that I was screeching Change I Need like '08 Barack Obama. Thinking and bleeding on the paved lot "Now you done got some." I had to split my philtrum to put progress in this Pilgrim, and I willfully admit my inadequacy. It's difficult building a habit when your mind's committing blasphemy. Inconsistency's been key to me, debauchery to decency, from crisis to see 2 things too equally, and it's unleashing unceasingly. I try to say what I'm thinking, but the toughy is not doing it deceitfully. But believe me, I'm deadly + serious, dialed in and delirious, I hop from track to rail, from Bon Qui Qui to Cornelius. And sometimes I want to build things indissmissabably conspicuous. Then ten breaths in procession that just sounds like an incubus. But now that I've jolted some of my CSF I've checked my DNS cause I hate when all of them get restless or are losing Interest. If I have learnt anything it'd be nothing. Yet nothing's <u>the impossibility</u> so I'm just unclean. Alas! Marriage is a little more than just a ring. A ringlet I can't be with for I'm not loving. I'm conceited, I've conceded, and Jesus, I'm coming. Sometimes you've got to bleed to know tomorrow's not guaranteed.

4/21/s **Twenty Twenty**
2020 suddenly wasn't everybody's year. We were having such fun then everyone confronted fear. All our peace is corrupted, what can we do but run from it? IDK about them, but I can't sit pretty like a succulent. Weakness creeps inside us like a succubus. To win we've got to burn her from within = ugly +

truculent. And hon, that is the sum of it. Upsets come from an utterance until they're shucking thunderous. And then all that worth troubling is what next will be humbling? Enter @ 2020, they think you're the ugly duckling. I'm a 2k baby so for me it's 2 decades coupling. So I'm donning this time upon me and used my purpose + drive as cufflinks. But dang! I'm spiritually hungry. And dang! My soul's stomach is rumbling. And the Biblios was Greek to me so now I study Greek. – 8-12-20
What's the point of new eyes if I don't open them? What's the use in loving people if I'm not showing them? What's the purpose of voice if it's not locution?

5/16/20

Heart says love
But my mind's made up
We don't need them
Because they don't need us
Yet why do they care
If I'm still cycling air
God loved me first
And now life's like a dare

May 17th – June 23rd, 2020

Le Mangling Finagling

He'd built it all. It had neat little shrubs he cared nothing about, and outdoor decorum to show off to people he wanted to scare off. The property was something he was really proud of. Although he hadn't changed it much, the acceptance and reverence of it made the house appear to be filling in the final slot in its landscape. The structure was one in which every sliver of its components was there on detrimental purpose. The layout, the volume, the aesthetics, the feelings of the house were all in perfect working order for him. Each inch was purported to invoke some memory and inspire some possibility. Potential and remembrance were the cornerstones with faith and hope being the frames. He saw all this perfect mayhem he had no role in controlling, and He saw that God is good.

She wandered on into the guarded grounds as if it was a neglected public park. Surveying surroundings and purveying opinions, she inspected. Whimsical and cynical, she slid her way into his graces. They did their best to be as honest as possible. They tried to relax whilst caring warily. He tried to secure the entrances but found her meandering through his house. At first, he treated her irrecoverably wrongfully like an eradicable anomaly. But his core corps had better orders, and he lent a hand as they trod down the halls. Through rooms with expensive views and closets with expensive shoes. Corridors with fresh blood on the floors next to torturous chambers then being restored. He introduced the investors and Nestors within. The sketchy collections and libraries of sin. Conformities, abnormalities, idiosyncratic, awkward dormants and Valerie. The dining rooms, the attic, the basement, and all between. He gave her free-range and rearranged cause he liked his life being seen.

Yet he didn't truly trust her, cause he still had one thing complicated. Others made him see himself as the only part of the equation. She was sweet, and she was rare = so much younger and wiser than him. And he felt even more less ready to share the room where another had been. We think he wanted to love, and he wanted her fun, but he was a pansy and antsy and dumb. She had rooms to design and lots of people at her place. So he knew for her to develop he'd be the one to leave. Whether they'd weather well, they'd find out on the autumn's eve.

5/18/20
I know there's no "I" in We, nor is one in Us or Team. But we are only individuals, and last I checked, in that there are 3. It's almost like a trinity. Like in His image simple-ly. The bearers of infinity. This breath is so wonderful, but we must breathe it trickily.

5/31/20
God is softly drawing me
By the filaments of my existence
From behind

He waits for me to 180
That He may make my
Faith be Sight

Fantasy
Futility (mwa) Future
FEAR

7-29-20 Business Exposition

This project enacts the finished product of a process that was begun this time 3 years ago. I was still a junior in high school, and my parents encouraged me to gain a head start on some sort of degree program. My initial and remaining plan is to pursue writing as a career, but I chose a business program, considering it to be the most versatile and adaptable to whatever I may encounter. Over my collegiate course, me and my family and friends have faced a myriad of hardships and health problems. So a major lesson I've been consistently developing has been endurance. Each semester was harder than the one before, and I had many times where I wanted to step away or take breaks. I even considered not doing this final assignment since I would pass either way. But, as with every struggle personally and academically, I have been able to overcome with the help of my faith, my family, and my fervor. My inhibitory tendencies are to either see what's before me and miss the macro-view or look too far forward and be blind to my next right step. The past couple of years have forcefully coerced me to slow down and be methodical and intentional, but also how to ignore my surrounding circumstances and inner distractions to crack down and focus on the tasks at hand. I have acquired varying degrees of knowledge from each of my teachers and individual classes, and they have all demonstrated a unique angle of the essence of business. One concept that has continually impacted me has been the idea of business as a balancing act. Every aspect of any sized business is like a strand in the web, and you can't manipulate one without influencing another. And whichever companies or small businesses comprehend this concept the most, they are the most capable of weathering internal, external, or economic storms. Communication is the key to success, to keep the business relevant and efficient. And along with all of the other systems and styles of business and management I've collected, I understand that these ideas are personal as well as inter-relational. We conduct business every day and not just monetarily speaking. We engage in transactional conversations and relationships. We learn to compromise and develop systems of our interactions. We manage ourselves and network so as to make ourselves more productive and secure. We reason, negotiate, downsize and upscale, analyze and innovate, and we do this every second of every day. I see that business itself is more than just reading and profiting from the market; it is a philosophy, a way of seeing life and living life, and I am truly grateful and proud to have studied it for this highly impressionable part of my life.

4/3/19
Making Daily Prayments

5/24/20 5:31 A.M.
I had to write this while it's un<u>adult</u>erated. The shadows we played with, the towns that we raided. The concepts we divulged, the removal of blindfolds. The rib-cracking laughs and the retelling of pasts. Shared hopes and dreams stirred with smiles and mood swings. I think Jonathon needs a monogram bumper sticker on your car. Neither of us see clear in a mirror so we see empirically peering at shards. Well, all that you said to me is lost in my memories. I feel for you in every respect of me. We have every right to connect except chemically. God made us separate yet the pressure is exceptional. Controversial like Brexit and sometimes sketchy like the Breakfast Club. Rebels with a lost cause living what's not socially acceptable. So let's reject affection and spend time like it isn't plentiful.

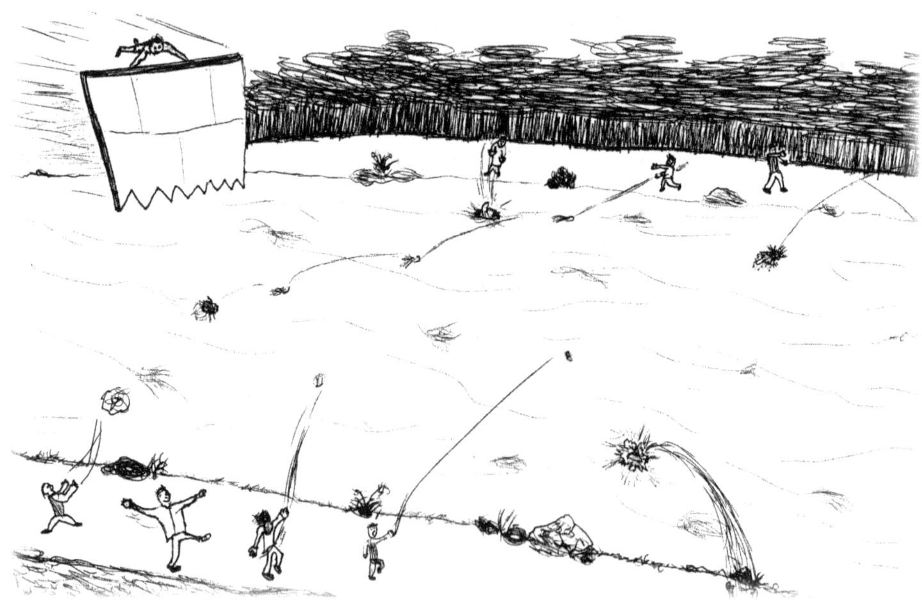

Figure 24. Tide of time

5/22/20
Segmented sectors with levels and Hoover Dams of confidentiality were given my consent to supposedly keep me safe. From everything that can save me, to choose the lesser of two mistakes. Succumb looks like surrender and trust is a transaction. Encouragement's discouraging when your purpose is lacking. My specialty was not matching. The loner's now a goner, but at least Homer's not a father. Self-awareness makes me careless; all the good times get lost like hairpins. Friends are gambles, so I only sample. Love's a concept I just can't handle. I won't share my identity, although I know it won't end with me. With everyone I act the opposite; will I ever conquer it? One side way to find some peace is self-regulated anxiety. To no one, have everything I told as insurance for my image control. I want the -ships, I really do, but I'm still so scared to follow through to gain and lose, to think askew, I'm entirely IMMOBILIZED. My emotions seemed like they were fine until my body wouldn't let me cry. "You can't pick and choose, they're all aligned." So I see my being happy was simply a lie, as was my belief I was satisfied. I'm stymied, I'm stifled, alone, at a stalemate. Everyone weighs on me, but I self-suffocate. I plea to God, but He knows I don't trust Him. My toilet is full, but I guess I won't flush it. I'm stuffing crap in and expecting gold will come out. I'll live in every moment except now. And it really irks me when I get stuck in a cadence or sound or whatever, just when I'm stuck. But then when I'm moving, progressing I get scared and brake. There are so many voices, opinions, theories; copious feelings, beliefs, systems, ideas too much even for Siri. So many things I should learn, but I miss them. I love me good rhymes and consistence in meter, but I know there's a better way: to say it without either.
Oh, look at that, another page of complaints. I hate my selfishness but not enough to change. My self-help suggestion box is worth more than Bezos, yet it's so big and full it won't fit on the payroll. Writing sure nourishes me to the marrow. Is it simply an escape for me ever so narrow? The best I could

write's down the drain of my shower. Yet I give it my best for some sense of power. I'd be fine with being like Eddie Bauer, with everyone knowing your work but not what you offered. First of my kind with a singular mind, another honorable Chaucer. References are just meant to put bridges in heads, but I'd preferably jump, swim, or begin climbing. Not to be seen cause that infuriates me, but to postpone the child in me dying. I'm an inheritor of heaven, yet my thoughts are hellish. Insufferable until I make my 3rd person jealous. I'm not sure if I like changing on the daily. One hour at peace beyond all understanding. The next, streaking, screeching, and flailing. I'm so selfful, I lie to myself that I have a right to be. And I'm so insecure I'm sure that my future has no bride to be. People tell me all the time I'm good-hearted and different, but He hasn't made me and them understand that all they like is Christ in me.

6/9/20

Emotional Dysfunction

6/29/20 – Lol – Proooooooof

(Wars Within + Out Myself)
I pledge allegiance to confusion and malfunction
Magic abdication and still I stand corrupted
Cyclically I lie saying I want God
To show me truth
But I run and run and run cause I don't really want Him to

7/10/2020
I am not attracted to you
I don't want to attract you
Cause it's worse to have a lie than a sad truth
It's worse to live a lie than a sad truth

That is true and not polite, I just don't want to psyche ya.
I'm simply scared you'll cut my strength like Miss Delilah.
The more time I've spent with you, the less I've been with Messiah.

6/18/20 – Insert lightning excerpt
My thoughts are too groggy. Everything's wrong. My neurons aren't turned on. I yearn for a turn on. I'm burning in her arms. I thought I'd learned a lot, but I learnt wrong. The past few moons I've lied awake trying to cope – with a pain that's self-inflicted and the reaping of what I've sown. I so wish I could cry instead of trying to force-feed or striptease my eyes. I don't understand anything so nothing of mine's concise. Here's a piece of my heart, no, seriously, here's a slice. I've been lying my whole life hoping for that bolt to strike.

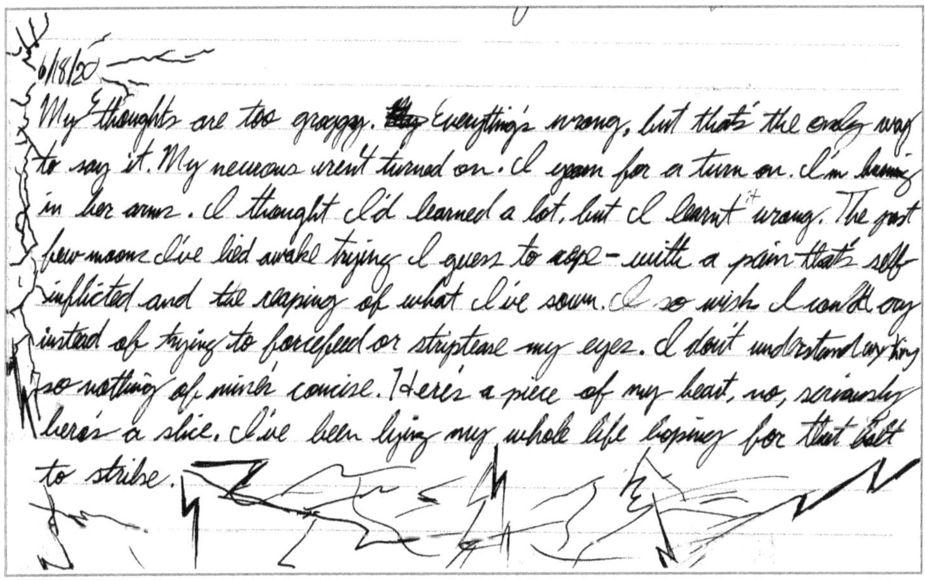
6/18/20
My thoughts are too groggy. Everything's wrong, but that's the only way to say it. My neurons aren't turned on. I yearn for a turn on. I'm burning in her arms. I thought I'd learned a lot, but I learnt it wrong. The past few moons I've lied awake trying I guess to cope – with a pain that's self-inflicted and the reaping of what I've sown. I so wish I could cry instead of trying to forcefeed or striptease my eyes. I don't understand anything so nothing of mine's concise. Here's a piece of my heart, no, seriously here's a slice. I've been lying my whole life hoping for that bolt to strike.

Figure 25. Lightning

I wrestle mania. There're things and feelings I want to clasp. But there's my heart in God's hand, and we both know He gets the final laugh. My whole life's a discrepancy fraught with violent tendencies; constant confrontation and consistent contradictions. I live in the moment and love it so but know something's missing. I find it when alone, but then I know life's meant for living. 6/29/20

7/2/2020

The Burden and The Blessing

Please believe this guarantee = This letter addressed to
Me = T-I-M-O- Timothy
In life, people are going to leave. In time, they come,
People are so much like the sun.
It shows up so unexpectedly if you like the night and
There find energy.
The dawn may shock you or it may crawl, but eventually
It will warm your walls.
The sun may play with you and share its vibrance, and
It always shines brighter when you invite it.
Though clouds congregate and your time will obscure, you
Will recount and smile on their tenure.
The rays may feel great on your skin and feel worth it, but
Return to the shade, and they just may have burnt it.
When people talk about people, they're unfair judgements, cause
They don't know them with you, they just know assumptions.
So when it's our star that you want to shun, remember
The Burden and The Blessing
Are One

7/15/20

Completion. Submission. Time to renew your subscription. Give me that confounded diploma or I'll give you a 9mm prescription! I'm only kidding in a way. New angles on faces and a new face soon on the way! A myriad of changes and IDK why, but God's being so gracious. I've got my Yoda Hut and its potential's on the rise. My sticky notes have clothed my desk with tips to write some beauts. A couple weeks and then I think my thoughts will finally cut loose! Peoples' ingenuity spikes when it's their default, but I love being alone cause then I'm creative without needing prompts. I want to write all of these subjects and publish so people can catch up. But all these hopes won't go as planned
and to that I need to fess up.

7-24-20
I'm privileged to be one of God's accessories. He's outwitted and twisted fate into a melody. I haven't learnt to harmonize and yet They 3 accepted me. It's funny how I need to die to find out my life's destiny.

I have no worry cause in this dying earth I am secured: For He's my Legacy

7-30-20
Imagine an entire generation that wants to be like their dads.

8-12-20

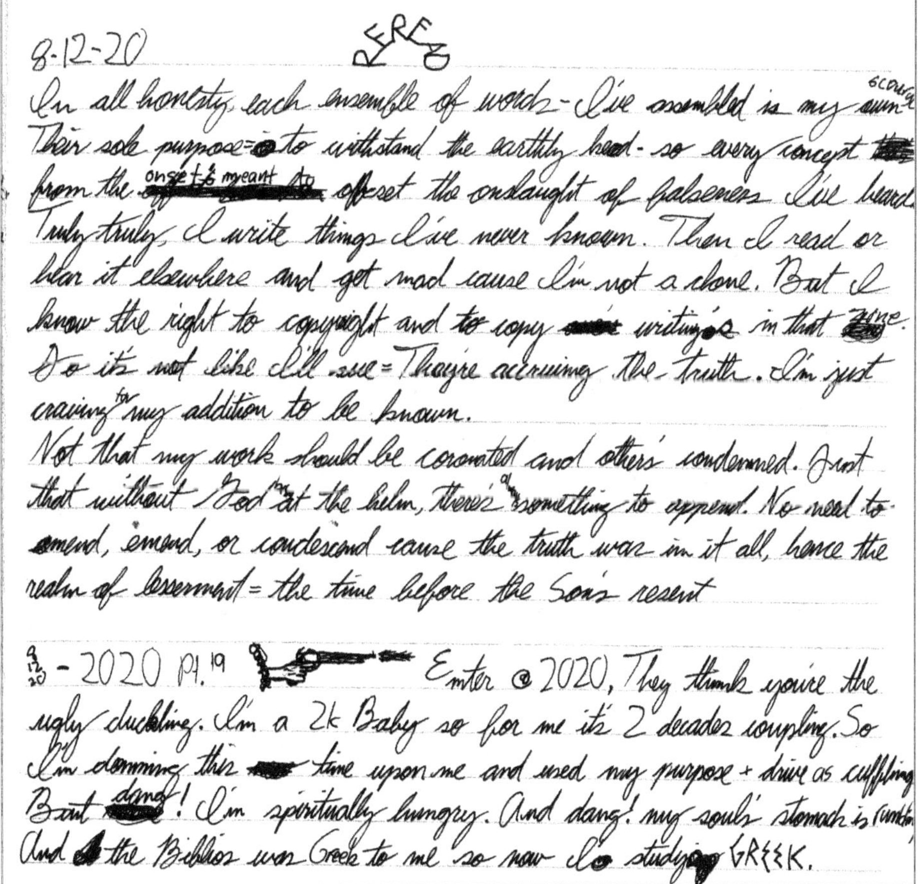

8-12-20 REREAD

In all honesty each ensemble of words - I've assembled is my own
Their sole purpose = to withstand the earthly head - so every concept
from the onset is meant to offset the onslaught of falseness I've heard.
Truly truly I write things I've never known. Then I read or
hear it elsewhere and get mad cause I'm not a clone. But I
know the right to copyright and to copy writings in that zone.
So it's not like I'll sue = They're accruing the truth. I'm just
craving for my addition to be known.
Not that my work should be coronated and others' condemned. Just
that without God on the helm, there's a something to append. No need to
amend, emend, or condescend cause the truth was in it all, hence the
realm of lessenment = the time before the Son's resent

8/13/20 - 2020 Pt. 19 Enter @ 2020, They think you're the
ugly duckling. I'm a 2k Baby so for me it's 2 decades coupling. So
I'm donning this time upon me and used my purpose + drive as cuffling
But dang! I'm spiritually hungry. And dang! my soul's stomach is rumbling
And the Biblios was Greek to me so now I study GREEK.

Figure 26. Reread

In all honesty, each ensemble of words – I've assembled is my own scourge – Their sole purpose = to withstand the earthly herd – So every concept from the onset's meant to offset the onslaught of falseness I've heard. Truly, truly, I write things I've never known. Then I read or hear it elsewhere and get mad cause I'm not a clone. But I know the right to copyright and to copy writing's in that zone. So it's not like I'll sue = They're accruing the truth. I'm just craving for my addition to be known. Not that my work should be coronated and others' condemned. Just that without God being at the helm, there's always something to append. No need to amend, emend, upend, condescend cause the truth was in it all, hence the realm of lesserment = so welcome to the time before the Son's resent.

8-25-20

My two-year tenure; one of fear and disarray
Yet His peace will endureth as will my lack of faith
When I can't cohere my arrears it will appear as disbelief
To be vigilant or vigil only with action is vigilante
Besides, "dis" means apart so is it to misbelieve?
I brought "love" with me, it tripped, it fell
It ran, I chased, and once I caught up, I knew not what I beheld
A patient first-mover, firmly permeable, indiscernibly discerning man
Independent, reliant entirely upon God's nonexistent plan
Hater, connoisseur of words which discourage and push him to live
Not "him," it's me, and I calmly dismembered him with a shiv
School's all I really left behind, cause it never cared for me
All else, I've a debt and I think it's for them I have been living
So what did I learn? What did I gain? I know future me will inquire
(I broke my emotions, so this one doesn't feel strong; I wish I was more of a crier).
Things will change, and it's great, and it's right, and it hurts

And I love this horrendous blessing I'm dealt
So to my times past, thanks and keep teaching me
To the unknown, see you soon, I am wishing you well

8-26-20

A moment of silence please. A moment for reflection. I think that deep down, I have a need for rejection. But everything just welcomes me with a warm reception. And I go on accepting it with no sort of objection

For Ezra

Coos and cries, your black fuzz, and blue eyes; the byproduct of love/ the original life. You stretch and you sprawl, you yell and you yawn, between your parents who dawdle and fawn. I've known your father for years and through ages. I hope you've been bestowed with his care-free, sweet, strength. I know your mother loves her boys, and you'll reward her faith. However much more you will be like your parents, I guarantee this to you: boy, you're in trouble! They're crazy and faithful and fierce for what's worth it. But don't get confused, we're still kids, much like you. We think we know what we want, but our needs are much greater. We think we're fine alone, while in another's embrace we're safer.

9-3-20 = Originally written on a hunting trip with Uncle Jon in Fall 2019

Here, I'll try to write it.
The heat is ultraviolet.
The wind is swimming lightly.
The cold is slowly biting.
The aroma's so inviting.
Trees atop Earth's head so plentiful and spiky.
Ope! The suspense is rising!

My, the wild is timely!
Birds hang out within sighting.
Turkeys like eagles, eyeing.
Up the food chain we're climbing.
From our lookout we're spying.
Hoping for something worth sniping.
Our relationship is ripening.
All the fakers for us are stifling.
For the weekend we're idling.
New memories for filing.
Savage, short mag 270, we rifling.
Into scripture so Bibling.
Becoming like Jesus so Christening.
Out here in nature we're wisening.
Once again the tension is heightening.
Here with Johnny, but no Shining.
Just one bullet, Barney Fifing.
But shaky foundations make me repine.
My level of trust in us just declined.
But no matter, cause for the TRUTH both of us beeline.

9-11-20 = 4 years using this book
I need to live as if I'm not being seen. *(separate)*: Nearing the final pages, I feel similar to how I began: Dispassionate yet adequate, dismal with potential, limited tho acquitted, so freaking selfish.

This little hand-me-down, Staples bought, easily replaceable book has been the tool God used to keep me on this life thing for 4 years now. It was not C.R. Gibson® who made this beautiful book. 'Twas the cosmic crafter Himself who fashioned the tree and creature and assembled and bound the parchments and protective covering. And it is still completely He who filled its lines with nonsensical perfection.

In all truthfulness, anyone who does read this (good dang luck!) will never care even remotely as much as I do about what is written within. And jeez, I try to read some of it years later and I'm either blown away by how relevant it still is, or I'm squinting and cringing attempting to remember what I meant. But each stroke, squiggle, scratch, scribble, smear, stain, and blot means an unquantifiable measure to me.

There are certain selections in here that would be realistically labeled better than others, but that would likely be because they are more palatable and profitable if they were to be shared. Yet, every excerpt is a testament to where I was at one time. All the attempts to rise above my fears and regrets, all the logical reasonings I'd never seen in such a light, all the confessions and apprehensions, all the weird wordplays that don't always add up but sound cool, all the questions… and the ?'s they incur, all the words that have been written have been revelations of the grace, might, mercy, and Love God has power-washed me in.

I had this hope that writing would simplify my thoughts and assist me in systemizing my reactions and validating my proactions. But after all this time and energy, I realize it makes me lean less on my own understanding and trust a Being that becomes more a mystery to me every minute. Writing shows me the war when I once thought it taught me how to fight it. Documenting and speculating are the identifiers of the battlefield. The battlefield where the victory is won in Christ, the holiness is harbored by the Father, and the validity is in the Spirit's presence. The spiritual war where we get to play a magnificent part, pre-defined and pre-reserved. We are soldiers. We are servants. We are children. We are adopted. We are heirs. We were bought with a price. We were dead. We are alive.

9-6-20 The Ballad of Fast Jack McLasky

Prompt: Fast Jack is a multi-faceted, unmatched in unattractiveness, unlatched, unhinged, and unfastened crack addict with all its additives..

John Everett McLasky was born and reared, by a tough-as-nails lady where the Trail of Tears, had been traversed not 20 years before...

Now stubby baby Jack always asked, "what's that?" and quicker than a flicker and a'faster than a snap, he'd be across the room to see what was in store...

But see his brothers and his sisters were not so inclined, they spent their days at a snail's pace and stayed just fine, but little Jack, he found them all to be a bore...

Jack's poor mama didn't see it as a gift, that her boy could run a mile before her eyes would even lift, so she set him about to do all the hardest chores...
It was the worsest form of torture to man the plow, and ole Jack looked up and he wondered how, come he was the one cursed with this burden for?...
For 18 years did he trudge like that, he was his own chain gang and at the drop of a hat he would break free to see if there was something more...
Then along came his chance when a hunter of a bounty, who was looking for a man who ran to another county, offered to take Jack along for a little tour...
Jack was ecstatic and asked what should he bring, the hunter of the bounty said whatever he'd need, and was taken aback when he packed no jacket, shoes, or horse...
Over time he found out why, cause this crazy kid Jack could run day and night, and after 35 miles he wasn't the least bit sore...
After the hunter found his man and got paid, he told Jack, "You oughta run for the rest of your days," and they moseyed over to find a job at a local store...
News spread quick about the boy who was fast, and before he knew it opportunities stacked, cause the world had a problem and old Jack he was the cure...
Across the country spread rumors of a ghost, who zipped its way from coast to coast, and only stopped to get a cup of water when it reached each shore...
Well though Jack wasn't the businessman type, he was a monopoly in his own dang right, delivering letters across the U.S. door-to-door...
Before the trains, Jack's competitors wanted the West, and their best bet to combat him was called the Pony Express, which they hoped and prayed would maybe even the score...
One rider returned, dismounted, and staggered, spoke of how he'd been passed by barefoot Jack who said his horse looked haggard,

and as he was left behind his heart was filled with scorn...
Along came another rider who said that he'd retired, and when he told what he saw they called him a liar, cause he said he saw Fast Jack outrun a snowstorm...
Alas, the final rider laughed as he drank, they asked if he'd seen Jack he said, "I saw the skank, I watched him race a jackalope and beat it so bad it went and hid in folklore."

Figure 27. Pulled apart

9-22-20 On September 19 – 20th

There'll be no excluding the mishap on the highway or the potentially fulfilled prophecy that precluded it. The/any interstate is already a gully of accidents waiting to happen, which channels all of my physical, mental, and emotional capabilities into a hastily draining funnel. Add to that the oft' accurate apprehension I am occasionally plagued with, along with an acute level of exhaustion from almost single-handedly packing my sisters' family's belongings and the toll of about 3 hours sleep following a viewing of Tenet, and you will be near to my feelings zealously surpassing those of reluctance. Thus, the predicament ensued. I was [(dare I say) miraculously] quite nearly squashed by a semi in the "crash valley" gorge in Tennessee. A chase proceeded and after probably 30 miles, a highway patrolman "got" him. But it changed nothing about how much it messed with me, though I couldn't notice it at the time.

Once we arrived at their new home, I cried soon after. Tho I was accused of being on drugs*, it was such a visceral moment for me. It was the first time in many months that the pouring forth of my emotions was able to overflow out of my ducts. Relief and Release are what come to mind as I remember how it went down. The rest of the evening I was in recovery mode.

That night, my dreams warped me into my time at 15. The vividness of my emotion-charged dreams are almost matched by the lividness I feel when I wake up unable to return, incapable of forgetting. <u>My emotional level fuels my impactful dreams and memories.</u> This set me on an interesting course for the next few weeks.

The following morning, I awoke really revitalized and excited for a more peaceful drive. I said my goodbyes and took my leave. I stopped at the nearby skatepark and what a holy experience! The weather was factfully perfect: chilled morning with a warming sun cascading through the discolored, falling leaves being cradled by the well-meaning breeze. There were

8, 9, and 10 year old's everywhere using scooters, helmets, and pads with one kid sitting on his dad's board: all under the careful observation of their parents. I was under the parents' scrutinizations, but I got to chatting with one and we really hit it off. Such a great time. Felt like a middle man.

Once I started driving home, it was just healing therapy with the open window, Strokes, and Jim Croce. Just peace. It was nuts. In one small town, I passed a guy (I believe homeless), and felt I should pick him up. I wrestled for a sec cause I was vibing so hard, but I turned around. I swear it was a test cause he was gone, and I looked but no luck. So I continued on home seeing beautiful scenery and gorgeous homes, and when I got home, I pet Cali a lot. I threw my crap all over the place, got a perfect NC apple out of the fridge, and took a nap in the SC sun.

Hands down, one of the most excruciating, yet rejuvenating few days of my existence. Then I packed up to head West.

**discussed elsewhere*

9-25-20 (originally spring 2020 at church)
It's healthy and refreshing when we lose our confidence.
Does it not make you soggy or itchy to talk on this?
I presume the way is to break away and be blessed on a later day.
Then jubilee is what you see as whirlwinds disseminate.
Separate:
Hold on. Since when did we become people with people rings? Fill the blank with your own name, but I won't be another of your furnishings. It's bad, I'm sure, yet I love intruding on people's lives. I might fail, tho it's worth the chance to be in your thoughts twice. Humans aren't just things that cross our lines of sight. We aren't anyone's casual passerby. We're the same, unimaginably, you and I.

10-6-20
I want to rest in the Finality of God. **Y E S**

10-9-20
"Man is a one-stop shop: you got fuel, ignition, transmission, and emission." – Me, quite tired

10-20-10
Would Satan interact with us if it didn't spite God's love of us?
Satan puts sin on sale when your soul is surfacing.
But even when we buy it Jesus still says we're worth purchasing.

- Please Lord! Don't let me figure it all out to then live none of it

To the tune of "Ode to the Mets" – 10-14-20
Biting your thigh... Biding my time... Coming to grips... in mid-July
I'm under your spell... latched on your wrist... wrapped 'round your finger... Clenched in your fist
Should you let go... I'd teeter and trip... I'd think it my fault... I'd want to get fixed
When the feelings return I will start to relapse
Sit with my back to the cliff with no seat back
Wanting to lean back Wanting to relax
Take a look at my heart
"No, I don't need that."
>?)+<".`&)
Perchance
You'll return from the highlands
Cloaked and shrouded, scythe in hand
Sent to precurse
My one chance
At the well of
Recurring dreams and resentment
Of the things that could have been
Youth and lust and contentment
Instead I commit all seven
Lent an ear to myself then
Lost
Them
All

Figure 28. Ode to the mess

10-21-20
Let's play a game, myself and I.
Okay! I spy............ pride
I? Can't find it? Cause it loves to hide
Vindictive, manipulative: from in front or behind
Lip service with its mouth closed,
It's the joystick to our eyes
For reclamation of your life
It tries. It fights. It cries.
We may seem brackish when it steals our luminescence and brine.
Some think we're not born with it, but it's our spirit's spine.
Quadriplegia's key, hearts broken and contrite.
Luckily and clumsily, I found the cure for mine ;)>
Some additional random thoughts:
-Against all odds. Against our God. We can always justify what we want.
-I care not to look better to do less
-Honoring God better when I get my way is a lie

11-19-20
You did it, didn't you? Convinced yourself of all the next steps correcting your missteps. You have got the form down; you'll nail it on this rep. So strategize and verify the path that's already been set.

My heart and soul writhe for the family and the man to be.........

11/?/20
Suffer -> Struggle -> Surrender -> Succumb -> Suffer -> ....

11/29/20
Father God,

Make me see myself as I am against who You Are. Awaken my days, Oh LORD, with the truth that I can do nothing to bring you nearer or make you more proud; only that I have and always will fail you alone who offer your Son alone who alone is able to retrieve me and relinquish my sins by becoming the receiver of the wrath intended for me. And it is now, each moment I exist here, through the power of the resurrected King and the leading of the Holy Ghost who indwells me that I live in the freedom of He who loves me so.

Praise be to YOU

- The object of your restitution no longer your retribution

12-2-20
Distractions plague me.
Infractions made me.
Detraction is my new form of loving safely.
But, Lord, I adore the scattering vastness amassed in the case of nature; your gifts to supply our every need both fortify and endanger. Each time I look in the mirror there's someone more foreign than a stranger. There's a type of peace that comes from knowing there is no pain cure.

12-3-20
L – is for our dirty laundry
O – is for the open wounds that bleed
V – is vanity, vanity, living in insanity
E – is the even score so when we leave we can be sure that

Love is nothing I can give to you
Love is an ugly, unsteady truce
Two in love can fake it
Take my heart, in bars encase it
Love's what unmade me and you

12-17-20
It's debilitating = Him killed is saving guerilla's detonating grenades with their AK's waving and kids parading brazen in curated masquerades serenading Satan. Yet by His Grace our Faith is situated. Our Hope's alive only because Christ awakened. Father's insatiable Wrath has forever been reparated. We're His workmanship, so now The Spirit facilitates it. The manifold Wisdom which capitulated. The bride-to-be are we, thus, of the cup, love, will you take it? Triune God, I ask of thee, why is Truth so manipulative? Oh yes, we want to be like You, so we said "sure, we'll taste it." So we ate it, saw we're naked, and now we know what happens when the sin nature has invaded. He made us to be with Him, so our "no thanks" left Him aching. I don't know for anyone else, but I don't want my Hope dilapidated. I want my eyes to close for the last time and open to His congratulations. But there's no way to be good and faithful when to service I'm not acclimated.

12-19-20
... and still this book calls to me. I wonder if not writing is my form of "to him who knows the right thing to do......"

1-4~~~10-21 Fast talkers gone quiet

Hello Everybody! Let's see a show of hands. For all who would rather complain than come plan. So you really don't see the intranet caravan? Oh, they do, but they really don't have or give a ($*)#*$. How could there be no price to join that massive wagon band?

I look at it as everyone is out on a beach flying a kite. Staying stationary, ignoring the impending night. Loving what agrees with them, listening with someone in mind. Always picking the coin but choosing from its two sides.

Therefore which one will we be looking at when we die?

@##$&))*&^:"&^

I lie almost the time all – 99.9 like Lysol – my insides fall – I need Midol – Sometimes I hit a write stall – then I try to reply all – I just wish to go home, like Bond in Skyfall – Do I really need a partner like in Spikeball>

1|7|21

God is not my tagline, punchline, and I'd better just acknowledge Him at the bottom line. My whims. My will = filth. I must ask great questions not give perfect answers.

1-26-21 [Before Longboarding an XL hill]

I don't want to be scared of death
Or scared to death
Or scared at death
I just want to be scared that death...

2-26-21

Doesn't know what it is to feel me
Inheritor of The Kingdom and heir of the King
Only by and through Him cause I've done nothing
By any means
Death is a locked door, my friend, and life, it is the key

1-11-21 – 2-8-21
Silent screams. My spit in streams. No hiding it, biding; no more I think's.
My dog's dying.
What a morn. Premiering before our Christmas post-postponement. She couldn't walk, her head was cocked. I held her in the garage. Mom and Dad made preparations; when her leash jingled, she stumbled to the gate elated. Sprinkles of sadness, madness, and turmoil intermingled within/amid me. Mom kissed her goodbye in the trunk of the Jeep. It all happened so fast; it wasn't right on any level. I held her head as she nestled and peered, her knowledgeable brown eyes acquiring some sun. the prism of her blue, purple, yellow in fur as black as the ink which I spend. Contrasted her spirit with the surroundings appearing in the white on her chin.

My eyes harbored water swiftly and my thoughts took time off speculating of the future unclear. Multiple times I fought back to the blessing where presently I could then say, "She's right HERE!" We felt the time fly, 3 years past half my life, she was firm while my world upended like a hyper-speed gyro-sphere. She loved to be loved and hugged and rubbed and run. She'll forever have her ball nearby. Her mane and soft ears, her flexible neck and squiggly tail, her gruff growl and smooth cheeks, her guttural exclamations and swaying rib cage, independent mannerisms and dependent demeanor, her humor and angst. We could learn from her a lot of adopt-worthy character traits.

She knew something was wrong but was strong to the end. The doctor said "She's gone" in my arms, and my heart's been bleeding ever since. I drove her home, I dug the hole, I carried and buried my friend. And my existence was burdened like a reminder of all I have sinned.

Her cumbersome limpness, her in my grip lifted, my chemicals between honored and abhorred shifted. The walk across the yard made her weight so much more grand. My whole body trembled; her body clutched in hand. I stooped and laid my sweet girl – ebony on red clay. I closed her warm eyes and then used all my might to stand.

"This is the hard part."

Dad, who's our rock, moved burial blocks; looked me resolutely in the face as he said it. For the life of me and the death of Cali, those words only served to abet it. He and I, on each side, with shovel in hand, were tasked with duty and deed to perform. Dad tossed the first scoop and her loose being recoiled from the debris. That red, nasty dirt contrasted her fur like meteors against grand expanse. I don't think I've done a harder thing with my hands. We encircled the mound with substantial stones. I couldn't believe what I'd seen, what I know.

"That was very brave."

As I sat in the corner that's what I heard mom say. If I hadn't done what I did, this "kid" would be a disgrace. She told me about Budgie (I almost forgot his name). But it was hard to not act like I was bleeding the rest of the day. I rode so many emotional waves when I slept my feelings sea had been drained.

Now it's not even the loss, it's the altered reality. When I open the door she isn't there to greet me. It snowed last evening, and she'd only beheld that once. Things have been fuzzy since then, girl, it feels like it's been many months. There's so much that reminds me of you, and you bring just as many smiles right now. So my <u>stinky</u>, baby girl, Cali: just to have known you once is enough to be proud.

12321

Who else hates the schism between what we say and what we mean?
Or how we live with what we know and believe distinct?
Of this I am certain = there are no certainties
Of this I am sure = there aren't assurities
Concurrently I yearn to be purged of my perjury.
So blissfully I listlessly
Hype Consistency is Key.
BUT
Wistfully
I itch to see
It's not
Consistently

2-10-21 (Excerpts from 6/25/20 + 10/10/20)

Earring Back (Tanning in the Moonlight)

I thought that you may, remember the other day.
When you stopped by our house to give my sister that plate.
But she was busy, and you came up to my room.
We got onto the topic of societal tools and their use.
Before long we were sharing our movie re-views.
And before even longer we were dancing to tunes from Footloose.
Everything we said was classic, like screenplays for Turner's.
Our age gap was nothing massive, neither of us were fast learners.
Then I said I hate to see you go.
She told me we reap what we sow.
So we said when we find something worth reaping, we'll be the first
One the other lets know.
As I ruminated and pontificated, the evening meandered by.
Then when I re-entered, an object caught my peering hand and eye.
The night was aged, but not enough to be wasted
And the sky was sharing its endearing stash.

When I called to see if she'd like her earring back?
She said she didn't need it
I said it's never too late.
She said she didn't notice, and I still don't know to this day
Did she let it slip off or did it rip off by mistake?
Was it The COIncideNCE of
Destined Freedom and
Twist of Fate**?**
Nothing should have power to get our mood right
Nothing Vidal besides black hair and blue eyes
We met up, and we were tanning in the moonlight
And we both knew
There would be
No tan lines
tonight

Figure 29. People of earth [4]

FALL 2018

MY

My Generation's the culmination of deprivation. This revelation which I'm relating desecrations and violations we're sadly stationed as close and open-nosed as we've exaggeration! Irritation irrigates the fields seeded of doubt and hate, but we're so but we're too augmented to imaginate. All we truly do is infatuate and then satur-Insects inspect the brain stem membrane. Feelers out for anything to alter faith. The altar's place. Pornography, technocracy, carnography, idolatry = welcome to it's more commonplace than complicators who conversate. What disorder affects subtly suffer from satyriasis. Emotion hoses no longer set to off just jet, high and But most of them are too deep in narcoma to become maudlin. Who else is scared by actors' soliloquies. No new nuances, humans are still nuisances. It's the same our hearts hope for conclusions. I doubt we'll get either in this leisurely exuberant just as many sicknesses as medicinals under guises like "well-fare" and "health-pendence. From Bel-Air to Belfair we're the underbelly of decadence. More kids our arms for dollars. We've been scissored, prisoners behind bar codes. No escape program QR Codes. Socially standardized and traumatized, as long as we're fed we' as long as the need to be met. Tick, tock, goes the Big Clock. What else to spend it 're feeding You. There's nothing Hollywood wouldn't do. Informing, indwelling, and es that won't come true. What the stars tell us is cool is just uncouth. We put all what love do. All these lies beginning with Elmo, held together with Elmer's; well, confide and compile that much more do we get confused. No matter how quiet or read, no methods or techniques, anything you choose will get us to the TRUTH. End may be a problem, but we're a solution too. Yet everything we need to need must to pick/choose? Enough of that rhythm. Let's widen the prism. Ultimately, we're as all time. If we're in the world, then we're in the wrong: on the wrong side. From most postmodern since the oldest garden, we'll be found fouling it up cause we're kind. His Son finished the sentence and made all faults alright. So when judgement we've tried and I've tried. None are acquitted. All are convicted who are not listed good night or write. Without Him we just connive when we should be contrite. To You give My Generation spiritual eyes. Please don't let us make THE mistake and the poverty line? When we've got closed fists and close grips for a robbery crime? jackpot, but the lottery's time.

Now the NEXT

10-11-21

GEN

is devastating. All formulations and evaluations equal to desperation. With all our ever been to conflagration. Oh, Yeah! And we're also the time period of over-genetically modified, all we can do is regurgitate. We think we use our imaginations ate, and when we're squeezed then we emulate. Then they, extend antennae. Sniffing sight and sound waves with hopes to alternate. Our eyes all on idols to take the information age <happy> Men copulate more often than women ovulate. Now guys alone, more than any others combined and diagnosed? I'll spoil it, we don't spritz. We're feeding a desire so insatiable we're growing incapable of cognizance. of being susceptible to gullibility? We're so far advanced, but we're still entranced condition even in these computer kids. Our bodies still need nutrition, and all of profuseness. Agencies corner markets, and it now looks like squares. Giving citizens care." We can fare-well and our care/health shouldn't be governed to points of de-cycle in, gossipmongers to wallow in squalor. Living in forgiveless systems twisting now, no breakout, no bail or furlough. We can't read books, but we can scan and ll scroll. Facebook Philosophies, Google is godly, and these monopolies will remain on when all you've got is Insta Intellect. Pull out your feeding Tube. Look what they' instilling since day one of our young youth. Distracting them with dreams and wish-our hopes in having someone say, "I love you." But we're so broken we don't know I'm coming unglued. I could complain for pages, but what's the use? The more we violent, we can't make or think our way through. Whate'er your self-helps or checks less issues to misuse and be remiss too, but I won't use any more to continue. We be infused. Because in this world of omni-options, how could we find what's right mankind as you can find. No matter any drawn lines, we're the same: depraved: for Mesopotamia to Laodicea, there's just been the bad guys and that God guy. To the offside. Since our hard hearts are insoluble, thank goodness He has one of the soft rightly comes seeking, in His blood we can all hide. There's no way to say it different in the killed and risen Lamb's Book Of Life. It's only because of Him I could have a be satisfied passing by Any person's standards should give us a fright. God, would be dismayed when faith is made sight. But what can we do when we're so afraid of These pearls won't get through all of your snobbery, swine. You've already won the

GEN knows exactly how I spent mine.

2-23-21 (10/10/20 + 1-21-21)
We are the leaders of the I Don't Knows - We are believers in what we say goes - But we're all so uptight now - And we're all so downright proud
People being what they've been told to be - People acting what they've been shown to be – People are starting to look like clones to me – So what people am I going to grow to be?
XXXXXXXXXXXXXXXXXXXXXXXXXXXXXXXXXXXXXXXXXX
I ain't a greaser and sure not with the sochs
I have spent the night with teddy bears and with roaches
I know that my life is not above all reproaches
I can't see in front of me, but I know where my Hope is

Was I spoiled?
First time around
was foiled, bah! Honest,
where lust once abounded
is a kid with Stockholm syndrome
in an abracadabra! Catacomb. His molindone
pantomimes to the Alamo. Alimony in calico like a salad bowl with Al Capone. Nonsense! Worthless! Nevertheless! I'm gonna word this cause it's all I've left! The knife fight ends. Love's like tridents. It punctures the heart and both lungs beside it, so you just bleed, not breathe, and in your profligacy you're deceived, you mislead and you're an imbecile to read...... My desires are so strong tonight for dark thighs, clavicles, with bruised cheeks on me only for you to console and hold me near, my head amidst your warm chest, our arms in knots, wrought together, your chin on my cowlick, our bare feet in a grappling match, we trace every langer

line on each other's backs. Every segment and measurement of your skeleton: I held and felt it. It's elegant. And every joint that's melded it: (my professional jealously wishes I'd assembled it) It's relevant. I hereby render your hair my hand's settlement. Every time we know us all, we surpass ourselves with excellence. When we kiss it is infinite: endlessness in its eminence. Short, little breaths dictated by innocence. Rhythmic, mystic motions calculated and dissonant. The part of me that wants to leave dies, deceased, and he isn't missed. I have described eyes, but I'll try it. They are ancient like papyrus? They steal my iitems like they're piirates? They leave clues in my mind, making eyeprints. I can't tell if they're gods or tiitans. They're teyerants. As in Cyrus with his empire, not to the Indus but two the Iris. Equal vibrance. Castor and Pollux = the Gemini alliance. Everyone she looks at become migrants. Full of wrath, power, and might, but gushing kindness. So much more to say and all behind your eyelids. Open; in their sight, I know that's where life is. Closed; makes me writhe, like I'm where the guy with the scythe sits. The vortex and the cyclone make a storm off the coast of Cyprus. I am syphoned, through the Einstein-Rosen Bridge from the island, through two time loops made by two tight ends. But ya know, that's just how it looks through my lens. Bravely courageous and still skittish. Couldn't find a weakness in you until ticklish. Silly thrillist, without a kill switch. I'll be your puppet my little ventriloquist. I won't withdraw from your class; you keep the syllabus. Until the day we get rigid ligaments; we gonna live it up like our final minute's imminent.

Figure 30. I love this one

2-13 – 3-5-21 I Love This One

2-14-21 (10/10/20)
2-22-21 – Ephesians 5:1
BeCome = as a child grows into the image of the parents, we are to be coming into the image of the in-finite Holy and Loving Adoptive Father.
Our Righteousness is as dirty tp to God.
But Jesus taking on our sin was a fragrant and satisfying offering to God.

2/26/21 {Bob Seger Song Style}
I've been in discourse… and I'm pulling my ripcord… It is discordant, I'm misinformed in the corridors… But I sense the importance… Cause if not for His Lordship… I'd be a sordid, corpse in, a morgue on the outskirts of abhorrence…
I thank you Lord for the connections…
But in the blitz of the storm, I thank you for redemption
And though I wrestle with the collection of the elect and the subsequent questions,,,,
Even then I thank you for-giving Love its Inception

I can't do it
I don't believe it
So Lord,
DO YOUR WORK
Why would I trust anything else?
Please
Please
Please
Cause it's not about my ability
It's cause of your cause and how
You willingly
Hang and gave yourself on the
Cross for me
Radiant Obedient Fragrant
Offering
The One Worthy to fulfill my
Measly, Puny

Desires
The One Who Died
Who took the might
Of the Wrath that was
Required

March
The 6th
Of Twenty Twenty Onety
Put your fire out on me, Yeah that's great
Covered in your pieces, I'm an ashtray
I'm just a -CENSORED-
Wait,
Am I that
-CENSORED-,
Either way I am the one they need to Castrate
That's just a joke aak?
So heterosexual I'm a magistraight
Ambidextrous, flexible, adventurous, effectual = like ballet
Sometimes I salivate, go ahead: retaliate.
Cancel me "out" of the caste system: the caliphate
Let's see the fruit of the root = it is the wrath of grapes

U N R E L A T E D

All that you spout's dire – So you're all outsiders? Outliers? "Oooooh, I don't fit in" = Did you count liars? Like Mrs. Doubtfire. So shout Boo Hoo. Like Count Dooku. I doubt you too, have had anything hard that you've been through. Here's the pity party train for you = Choo choo

Oh \Words\
When we gonna Learn \Words
All we care about are Works \Learn \Words
But it's all gonna Burn \Works \Learn
Burn \Works
\Burn

3 ÷ 7 ÷ 21 ≡ 5 ÷ 22 ÷ 21
Perhaps I'm the one to blame = I can take it
Urge lapse went and came = I can make it
I knew from the outset not to go that direction like Jonah
Like contra-Minerva, I went elsewhere from Nineveh
You were searching irksomely for the highest bidder –
whereas I was looking to be of service like a babysitter.
Additionally, indignantly I wanted to test check my love lever and its position. Distantly, you were living by "the opposite of love's indifference." Well...... Our cognizance was off a bit. Things didn't add up like economics. Mixed honest and reconnaissance into a two-piece monolith. The problem was they didn't wanna fit. Acting like we've got the Love of God but God Love Is.

That last statement was mightiful, I hope none of us missed it. Kid, we had no voltage = we weren't electric like Triscuit. I've had my heart's harp tampered with and it's still quite out of tune.

Now I see it was wrong of me to change your amp's volume.
And since I mentioned my trek West to reside by Colorado.
There seems to be an echo, and it's now a common motto.
But Silverado and Silverton show He holds El Dorado.
I was thinking, speaking regionally will show what I mean.
Though it seems like the mountain between us has grown to the size of Pike's Peak...
There's still one voice that hasn't shared, and I say we let Time Speak

3-9-21

Across the field of weed-veined pavement, from a dilapidated factory in the deserted, industrial side of town, runs a youngin like a fugitive with his backpack and hoodie on. He jogs with

hopes to leave this as a mention of his legacy as a discrepancy in the south, how he didn't wait and expect changes once he'd packed up and gone. All this and more! On his sojourn before the water-tower. This was the chance to show himself how not to cower. And that's not for the sake of rhyme. That's for the change of mind. That was for the rate of tiam. "This fate of mine" said he with his Vans laced, clomping on asphalt 4 times his age, in step with the rumble from the adjunct train. He lost the hoodie and donned a climbing harness. The bulwark was graced and braced as he approached its base and watched it stretch into the unscathed sky.
But he knew it definitely loomed larger in his mind.
Now, T.W.I.M.C., you may wonder why.
Why not tell what transpired? Well, because it's mine.
Wait, so which one writes? Is it "he" or "me" or "I"?
Well any which way you slice it, someone out there died.
Oh dear! Oh my! Oh Fear? Oh hi! No... Fear¿ Oh nice!
Cause post-mission there was no compunction. I sat apprehension in a chair, commenced to punching. Pretty soon the room was littered with chunks, and I learned a little something about the function of fear and how his cousins come near, latch on, and suction = make us a luncheon =
But here's the comfort: if you've got the gumption, steal a nightstick, and proceed to bludgeon. And for me, he's licking his wounds because that battle = I won it. And this time it's afraid of me cause we don't know what next is coming.....................................

3-Fiteen-Twenty Wun
<u>Excerpt from my privately shared journal</u>
... But I really do feel like I came full circle. <u>That's a LIE</u>. GOD brought me full circle. Pretty much against my wishes too ha! But I'm really seeing the battle between The Spirit and my flesh

still fighting on the field of Emily. The hardest part about it, too, is to win, I must surrender. Not the amazing memories, lessons, and blessings, but the attempts to change what He means for good (His good) into what I can only want for evil. None of it was mine in the first place.

All this in no way means I didn't nearly tear up at work yesterday like a newb, or dream about you and your family last night, or believe that 16 and 17 were da best. We were so naïve (me more 4 shore), and I was actually, factually, madly happy. Not many people get that treat. And I would've done anything for you, heck, I still would. Who gets to be that stupid and not have terrible repercussions? Hardly any man. We are freaking blessed kid. And that's about it.

It doesn't all need to be pointed out or at, just pointed to Him.

3-16-21
Why do we have to feel good?
Why can't we be good by feeling His goodness?
Why must we believe in peace and fight extremes?
Why can't we find a path from His radical balance?
The fact that He Is, irrespective of us is reason enough to fear Him. Add to that His Desire, His Want, His Will is to shower mercy and for us to be with Him. Talk about Fear and Trembling. The only disconnect is our nature, flesh nature, false nature = a sick replicant of an impossible perfection. No enlightenment necessary. All that is required is hopelessness, need, contrition. Not just the acknowledgement of it, that places us in sovereignty. Fear Him. Revere Him. Endear Him. The Impossible God. Undependent of us. Willingly, Eagerly, Immediately filling fully us with Himself. Fill-Full-Ment. That's what fulfillment was meant to have meant. When we no longer live in between Empty and Fullness? He can exceed our earthly limits. We just must repent. We simply need to believe

in He who is the only one worthy. We have all missed the cut, failed by a perfect standard. But it's not by our _____ that we come to Him. It's because He Chose Us.

"The righteousness of God through faith in Jesus Christ for all who believe. For there is no distinction: All have sinned and fall short of the glory of God, and are justified by His grace as a gift, through the redemption that is in Christ Jesus, whom God put forward as a propitiation by His blood, to be received by faith. This was to show God's righteousness because in His divine forbearance He had passed over former sins. It was to show His righteousness at the present time, so that He might be just and the justifier of the one who has faith in Jesus."

– Romans 3:22-26

3-26-21

I'm feeling those good vibrations. She's giving me inflammation. I wish I could stake my reclamation. I'd let out an exultation. Perpetual exclamation.

Have I ever been forsaken? Anyway, I'm in lamentation.

And now all my concentration, is on how I'm using this space I'm taking.

IN
R
E
S
P
O
N
S
E

In my estimation, that crap was defecation. Fulfilled none of my expectations, didn't make it past red tape or regulation, but I didn't do it for edification, and so here is the cessation.

4321 My Heroes

Well, that's a new one. Anyhoo, my parents are heroes for rearing a hoodlum. My childhood was a good one of contentment, affection, well-earned and well-learned lessons. For some reason they'd replenish me even with my disrespect and pretension. Irrespective of my rejection of their corrections, my adolescence was a collection of questionable perspectives and attempted insurrections. Discipline was my hate language, but they eventually got my attention. Amidst my sin retention and edging them to contention, we've been turning into what I think's a wonderful friendship.

They're so dang patient, it angers me. Sure there are slip-ups, mishaps, shenanigans, pull the slide back and chamber me. But those were the durpy precursors like Raimi's. We're so mature, but let's put it in reverse for a detour...

What word do I prefer? Reserved? Perturbed? Strict. But there's much worse to be. While other boys my age were getting cultured, I was developing me. I see now that getting your whims as a kid fulfilled isn't really living free. Freedom in any form has a cost, and that is responsibility. My mom and dad strengthened that half of me = is it not evident? If not, it shows more about how I've not been listening. Cause it shows in the kids when their parents kept giving in. The future holds the fruit of those rooted in discipline.

I was surrounded by church kids and conservatives, so explain to me how I'm most comfortable with lurches and undeserved? I'm fascinated and in the most antiquated of ways, progressive in nature. A sucker for the long-standing but with a firm stance on metamorphosis. All of this from my spectrum-spanning family. I'm parts of them, the good and bad, but all that to say I am so glad! In my pursuit of uniquity, I nearly enacted mutiny! On the truth, no less, stupid fool, You (Me)! But truthfully, and as I think this, I grin so toothily: my parents are my heroes.

They are knowledgeable = applicably so, honorable = for they've fallen so low, incomparable = seeing their role at the bottom of a totem pole, humble and soluble = dissolving suddenly = serving, yet lovingly = subservient, fervently = firm in the turbulence. Still irksome = concurrently. But the only thing that worries me =

Is if I don't learn from them.

Cause I take an observation and see how many errant parents' marriages are intact. I hardly know how to respond to that fact I can never retract. They say it's all thanks to God, and you believe it when you see Him act. And knowing why doesn't matter when He shows how He adds and subtracts. But my greatest gifts I've been given have to be my mom and dad.

4
10
21 on 1-18-21)
My flesh gets the best of me – I know my focus needs more focus, but Mr. Miyagi, my hobbies are obstinate hellishly – like I'm on the devil's telepathy – so here goes the death of me – dead to the promise of wealth and health and rejection of the card deck been dealt to me – I sin effortlessly – professional jealousy – on a free Cruz through life, Penelope – selfishly rebellious with every cell in me – regularly, cellularly LG, 4G, LTE – yet His excellence is repellant, incessantly – reverently I retell me and my soul selectively – Emergency! – yearning the entrance wound so I'm exiting the effigy – it's always on the offensive and my defense mechanisms are wrecking me – But secondly, He said as often as I take the cup and bread "Remember Me" – And it's about how it's not yet ended, to repent is splendid, His splendor's resplendent, and now His ascension means my soul's reception, only He replenished, every need has been quenched, and He's swept every blemish off of my complexion, not effort of mine, or sector of life, or by my confession, but just by His presence, by His ever blessing, by His very mention, by my own relention, then comes His cleansing of my every section.

Truth is not just objective, its service is not selective, go ahead and reject it, it's perfectly fine to suspect it, it's not highly respected, it's the school, not the class, thus, it's not an elective, when it's time to learn, we should say the truth is in session, so tune into the lesson, trust it is a blessing, I'm just messing, it's distressing, to our clandestine essence,
Entrant lieutenant colonel of second infantry regiment with no prior commission or commencement.

4-14-21 (context: Watching Dad nearly pass out watching Everybody Loves Raymond)
Time flies when you're laughing numb.

5-3-21

Always one step ahead or one step behind
For once I'd like to be in-step more than one
Step at a time
I think I'm sorry my hair bothers them?
Better not let 'em see my squalor then
Dad just came in and hugged me and held me. I told him I feel like I'm just running full speed = towards or from something. My soul feels constipated like my belly. I'm at a stand-still with this stalemate cause I'm never hungry. Mostly I'm thankful for the relations He's
Taking from my life
So so many mistakes I'm making cause I'm not
Grateful tonight

5/4/21
Like monogamy, a correspondent oddity is how knowledge afflicts, inflicts with conflicts. We're just pawns armed with songs on wits. With constant trilling it's bleak: we can't call quits, and in this age where "new" """""Information""""" appears king = we know everything about each thing and live nothing for anything. Smh at the phrase Guilt By Association. No longer of this world, thus un-patriation. When God says take up your cross, He means follow Him to obliteration. An

invitation to death sounds more like surrender than affiliation.
But do let's carry on with our trillion observations...
And don't squirm or cringe at the thought of our somber stations

ASININITY

Seemingly apathetic people are what I call Primary Care Givers lol
I am so contained and so controlled, it's despicable
So is everyone, even ones getting all political
Alone, as one, we're singular, collective individuals
_Principalities distracting, then trapping (it's not that difficult)
Make a mad dash like Mad Max insuring (Aflac) through fire
(Shadrach) for the backlash here's a trash-bag FIG like Dad's
snacks Sat in ash with sackcloth so here's an ash-sack.
_Me? A grunt, runt, frontrunning brunt of the joke
_Insidiously perfidious
Just over der, trying to manage my RAM
I payless, I could care less about the brand
Of the ilk that what's physical is a scam
_Cause I expand my wisdom less from them than a homeless man
Rage against the Machine Rage against the Nothing
When I was 14
I was swarthy
Everything was a sure thing
I don't know exactly when
But I got sent through a portkey
MAIKE them = thoughtless
Screw Institutes = Lawless
Don't Listen = Sophists
Refuse Truth = Flawless
Literally just random, good little bits that didn't seem to fit
-Yours Dually

6-3-21
I grew up in church doing mission work and there were some things I got to see – Try to map it out like I just took up cartography – But we'll have to go deep inside similar to colonoscopy – Only if you live by something can you have hypocrisy – Hoes have more excuse for mediocrity – Monotonic worship is a mockery – Motive/Motion = I malign monotony – Men and Women equally cuncockting – Knowing, yet not doing's such a novelty – And occasionally we see straight up apostasy – But let's hop over here, sorta like a wallaby – Gospel Corporations out sharing their policies – God's chosen children living in hierarchy – Instead of being bondservants they want to be the next Socrates – Instead of spreading honesty, let's fill opportunities with malarkey – Why be redeemed to then get lost in the bureaucracy? – We see heresy; Pharisaical: oftenly – Admittedly, we willingly clog the Biblical arteries and for what reason? A hard on? – Should I be sorry? Would you like me to beg pardon? – Since when should we trade God's favor for Theological Stardom? – For those who are truly born again = life is entirely postpartum.

6-12-21
That... was Zoroastrian. Anything but disastrous = emotion-motion sickness like the end of Prince Caspian. Sad, looking back, but in that passing, traveling, road-side attraction I learned a lot about life and why to keep it out the trash-bin. At the stop sign, coming off 25 onto 11, chatting with Landon with my raggy dew, smelling like a diesel fire and movie theater food, from right to left came a black Jeep, and I wish I could live in when our eyes meet. We held the other hostage it seemed, rendering them immovable apart from their cheeks. The randomness and suddenness is what exposed their teeth. Not lafs or primal instinct. But something so ancient and truer than deep. YET, the mystery is instantly morphed to demoralization. = Life is just that smile shared = a glancing wayside sight, that were you to try to see again, won't see you, try as you might.

6 - 7
8 - 27
21

Self Defense

To fully disclose and reopen myself, of that I am more scared
Than to leave all my dreams of accomplishments to forebear
Capturing thoughts as captive hostages, trying feebly to concentrate, not like Auschwitz. Trying without luck to be verbally observant. So I'm observing. Watching what I say so close, looking for the wormling.

"Pretty sure he spells Alleviate = Seclusion." Alluding to the illusion of safety = spake he in a trialogue. "It's true, I heard, he, Lucifer, and God." "Affectionate as an epithet, some wouldn't hold his hand." "Recollect like an elephant (he wouldn't rhyme with that; it's too easy.)" Where did the general keep his armies? Wearing his heart under his sleeve, feeling the need to keep your peace. Wants = to be alone / has to be seen.

In case it seemed encased, the general's me. Going through my writing has been eye-opening. What I grapple with today, I'd written years since. I still strain so irrepressibly to be not always better but different. But isn't different than better worse? (Notice how the subject looks at things in reverse). Conversations and comebacks I rehearse and rehearse...

Always outrunning suffering, yet I can still justify grumbling? Last year's dreams, I'm wondering, writing this, fighting it, thundering. Why do I start to give up being precise = like the Thompson's I'm bumbling. If I just call it what it is it's lust, and it's a cinch. It's like epilepsy but to masturbate's/ disobey's the twitch. It's like sticking the spear in Jesus's side and giving it a twist. He's freed me from this demon's seizure, but I leap back in. A maze of false humility and ambiguity in me smile. I've been entrusted with just enough to divert and beguile. "Women's exclamations and men's acclamations are skin in the game for him to bite." "HIS skin was in ribbons so that Tim could live in respite." But you never get to see me alone, he's hiding in plain sight. Info, lymph nodes, symptoms = my poltergeist is Pride. And any who Truly Love me will kick my face and aim me to

Christ!

That would've been a sweet ending, but the meaning must commence. Got to explain the title of this crappy penman's mess. The war is so effin' deceptive, it rages while you wait in suspense. No matter how trained I am, I am helpless to stop what I'm against. Only God can save me from He and me, He's zealous and He will avenge. It makes so much sense. It's not just dying to self, but His putting to death and giving Himself that's Self Defense. So instead of the newest cleanse, I just come to you, and I Confess.

Figure 31. Self Defense by Brendon Carson

BRITISH LOVE LIFT 8|16|21

She informed, "You're a nutcase."
I concurred, "I'm a fan of that."
She resolved, "You're an open book but a tough nut to crack."

Then with an inviting elbow, a gesturing hand, a slight bow, a light smile, following a tip of my hat: she nimbly grinned, curtly curtsied, and we laughed as we crawled in the cab...

Chapter 1

They were laffing sterically; the two, three seats over my starboard side. I could see them in the reflection of the window to my port shoulder: eyed. The brick lane kept me preemptively preoccupied, until I was aware she wasn't having a particularly smashing time. He was high quality, of fine colony, a man of great taste and class. I'd oft seen him, the mangy changeling = inside out he was the ($*)#*$ of an ($*)#*$. I would have been content simply on-looking, had she not blinked in such a wanting manner. Then I saw she was precious, and that her presence wasn't demanding or that of a commander. As if in servitude, she requested to be excused, and he'd see her again, or so he presumed. And as she walked with her coat, and he acted the goat, I calculated that I should use the loo.

Chapter 2

Once both water closet doors informed "vacant," we each stepped out, eyes cast down, like two vagrants. And when our sight aligned, it was as if souls were spliced. A hawser was being threaded and lashed together from separate ties. I don't recall the words uttered to convince her to take part; just my lungs turning to tongs and squeezing my heart. We devised a devious plan, the envy of any mischievous man. And when the next look-a-like came along, she departed with a perfect jacket first-hand. We watched the richened ruffian follow her out, bewildered and befuddled as he was. From the vehicle we saw him quibble as he found that he was played by the woman who had everything for him but love.

Chapter 3

We scoured the streets. What better method to meet? Than to tour life, guided, with that person on the next seat. Now it was our turn to laff, from Islington to Bexleyheath. The automobilist was on our side, and we called him coachman or bosun. He was our getaway driver should men in red or blue coats come. We crashed galas and blasted plazas, then we'd both run. Everything we did, lit by night's cold sun.

Chapter 4

For once in our lives, we were anything but in-step. As the evening creeped and progressed, we appeared the more unkempt, and once the monks left, we rummaged St. Paul's mare, more aware than e'er before of how and where we're inept. Lying beneath the murals and soffits, I scoffed at my abandoned, bland canvas of a day. But now I was here in this artsy atmosphere where every centimeter is ornate. She turned to me in a way that could never impress more grace, and she smiled in a style that makes storms break, and I realized nothing that had been beheld before had more beauty than her freckle-adorned face.

Chapter 5

Not that it mattered, but we were knackered by the night's end. And I'm so tropelessly devoted so we took the road from Brixton to Brighton. I reclined awake, but she succumbed to her eyelids. I paid the cabman handsomely, said he was brilliant, and he said he'd been delighted. Then she exited, but the ground never knew she'd alighted. In my arms she nestled close, her cold ear to my cheek. And with no haste, we made our way to the beach. Midnight memories made in the A.M.

synergized swimmingly. Lying against the cornerstone, the sun arose, and the immigrants went to sleep.

Thanks for letting me write this!

It is so simple and sweet!

Complete 9-7-21

(Making grilled cheese sandwiches at 9 P.M. with grandma) "I love doing things like this. I don't like being all regimented." – Dawn

8-23-21

I've been looking back so much my neck aches, thinking I'd better take a good look 'round. Everybody's proud, and I ride that wave till it drops down. Everybody's watching me so never wear that frown. Stifling the Spirit, hiding right in the mirror, underlining nearer to my underlying fear of pining my dear when I should incline my ear. Eager to hear but not stopping once I regain composure. Cause once I feel I can repose I dim His reflection...

...That was such garbage! What happened? You type it up, find some love, throw your skill in the trashbin? You've got no heart or skin in the game, you're just a skilliton? All these dummies like "Does he mean SKELETON?" No, Cracker, get back on your Peloton! I'm just aspiring to the likeness of Jon Bellion... lol. I know he worked his heaven-blessed butt off. I just want that purification that doesn't come off. The kind that rubs off. I want real success and to be with He it's because of.

I want people from my olden days to say:

"Look how far he's come."

I wish I had one of those stories like:

"He's finished everything he's begun."

"No one could match the pace of the race he's run."

But the fact is I'm just in pain like I'm Liam.

It's coming from my gut, it is intestinal.

Nothing by incidence, everything intentional.
Even contention, even when split like a sectional.
Even consensus? Even when sex is suspended I'll.
He's in detention. See him in the retention hall.
THEY THINK HE'S A GOOD BOY, BUT HE WANTS TO BE... ON FENTANYL
Readers be like, "He's a moody 'B'" hah
But don't sell me short like QVC hah
It's getting harder and harder to say what I mean yah
Pulled the slide and waiting for the hammer to fall like I'm Queen yah

Figure 32. Skilliton

I know my mind should be on the teacher and his mono-long (I meant monologue), but dear, your hair looks like a corsage. And you're not one I want to scare off or score on. But your demeanor and behavior I give five out of 4 stars. In a heartbeat I'd date you and take you to a courtyard. You're someone whose hands I'd appreciate on my forearm. But I'm also convincing myself that without you it wouldn't be more hard. For starters, I have much more to garner, and yes, I hear you, I'm not thinking of how to applaud her, or how we'd be as a mother and father, and there's just stacks of attraction I'm lifting, and I really need a spotter. I believe we'd pull each other harder, but when do I stop feeling like a son and take someone's daughter?

9|4|21 – Choice of good and evil like I'm little (Lloyd) Garmadon – Between the beginning and the End Or Alderaan – See them racing to the finish? Kid, we be sauntering – Slowing the flow of time, I'm Prince of Persia minus Iranian – F-Boyz "F" "B's" with no port for WiFey harboring – Watch what you eat = meal plan, cause a real man will be honoring – This more than writing a book, I'm starting a conglomerate – You Were Born at the top if you're reading this, then lend a hand – So would you rather withhold or withstand – I will remember who's been there from the start just like Krillin – I just want to be a man of faith much like Jim Hand – If God's won the victory, I'm not a contender then – And I can't just wander aimlessly like the Endermen – I've been privy to please and mos def offended – But I know I'll do both again when I type this letter and send it – Everybody has been a blessing with their advice and discretion – But guys, most of the answers after time multiply into more questions – So, correction = I thank you, you're beautiful, you're splendid – But leave me to freaking be when He's giving directions!

5 years of consistent writing
9-11-21
There's this groaning in me to be enlightened
But I just need Fear and that's why Jesus died then
Resurrected and in me He's Alive and
There is no better reason to be enlivened

Sep 16th – 21
"How can you say, 'We are wise, and the law of the LORD is with us?' But behold, the lying pen of the scribes has made it into a lie. The wise men shall be put to shame; they shall be dismayed and taken; behold, they have rejected the word of the LORD, so what wisdom is in them?"
Jeremiah 8:8-9
"Hola, I come bearing cashews" –
Dang it, some of you are allergic (achoo) –
Christians like to act like their carrying Bad News –
Or they coming at you with that knockout = Matt Hughes –
When did the "Gospel," become a job like Rockwell? – Trying to impel to "get well" to get to the following module – But I pray when you look into my fuselage there aren't bombs – no warheads or Corvettes just the joy of God………

<Based on 4-23-21>
Before I get this one started, would anyone like an amaretto?
I regretfully have to tell thee there is no such thing as equality.
My nose won't grow, it's not the craftsmanship of Geppetto.
For real, not even twins, and I'm not meaning this symbolically
=
How long do we keep fighting over Monticello?
Or what if Abel killed Cain? \ No real symmetry
Our only fair ground is our finity,
BUT UNTIL WE SEE IT WE KEEP CONQUERING ON

OTHELL●

9/
20/21

The
Way I Write

"What's your book about?" "What do you write about?"
"What's it mean?"
Weeeeeeeeeeeeeeellllllllllllllll, it's fascinating, facilely. A
construct of My mental faculties.
Just a facet of a fascicle. A product from
My mental factory.
Really? Really?
Rapping off the bat, I'm such a silly Willy.

REAL-ly, seriously I don't have answers to all my questions either, but hear ye, hear ye! This writing has changed my life. It's far more than a hobby, and it doesn't help me relax. By rhyming with a rhythm I find I live in a limited gap. Nobody showed me this thing I would love so extensively or excessively; I was just given the ability and the desire. The best question is HOW. Why? Cause How I Write has been my teacher for Why. But the reason I write we'll save for a later time.

I don't always rhyme, try as I might. It's just the structure and the sound off are really addicting. The breakdown and the breaking up are a sweet challenge I readily accept. Except for when I don't lol, I try to balance how much I stretch and exercise. Cause oftentimes it takes more strength to make a concept concise.

But I love to bake, making cakes with layers
Of Convolution.
Other times I torture my mind to find a
Simplification.
I don't want to get "educated" in writing cause I've seen people
Earn PHD's and lose IT

Just nourishing and nurturing my craft and staying
Uncomplicated.
I like my verity allegorical
I type the metaphysical via the metaphorical
It's difficult keeping different and not being deplorable
While acting in a cast where no facts are supportable
But accordingly I'm storing up, and I'll sell my shortage affordably
Only He can keep me priceless and timeless
So shelve me or helm me
Either way I'm excited.
Whether I expire or set fire
I'll always know
I tried it.
Finding diamonds mining deep in the coal
But the farther I dig, the harder it is
To keep word count low
Walking blind on a slackline
Between
Staying thorough and Retaining the soul
How could I be a
Goat or
Stallion
When this Colt
Acts like a Foal?
It's the opposite of "nose goes," it's "do I get to write poems or prose?" Shall I let go the tempo or set up the metronome? Or maybe a reference is a detriment if the allusion alludes to something unknown!
Sometimes

Just like that, I break character and narrate. Narratives are imperative if a statement's at stake. I hope to write full stories one day; it's a skill I'll have to develop.

But for now I'm fraudulent as a novelist.
Just Not A Fit
Like an author selling his/her novella at Coachella
In these short spaces
I write on God, it's
In court cases,
Or in songs, comics...
Oh, Wait! Check the gate! Did we just let one escape?
I wasn't supposed to say that...
Like the president being Honest when addressing the State...
This gringo's lingo's loco, writing his recondite abstracts.
This wedo's word es no soso, these matters so aptly rapped.
Won't be surprised if I climb the highest in S. Carolina
Like Sassafras.
But I bow to the giver of the gift who will
Tell me when
"That's a Wrap!"

9-24-21 – Too. I just had to get this one out:

<u>This One Really Needs a Title</u>

Self Help
Self Wealth
And Self Health
Meanwhile, I'm keen trying to Self QUELL!
It seems I'll, get senile in this realm.
Smugly running amok among this sucky crud (squelch!)
But I screwed that and threw that in-flames
And now it's starting to swell.
Everyone wants to be Goggins, but they won't wash the dishes.
Staying Hard – hearted, but the softness causes the difference.
Wanting to be godlings = acing all they own quizzes.

These idiots' divisiveness is what inhibits collective fitness.
Me – My
Self – I
Ours? – Mine!

But check it ---

All I write is news to me. That's why usually, I'm unimpressed by artists musically. Cause I get outta the box, I'm done talking cubically. But if none of it's new to you, (if you knew the news), why don't you live like you do? Why don't you put it To Use? It's cause In-Form-Ation is more than new news. Don't be sad about your inutility, these aren't blue clues. Make it fuel and make like a train = chew chew. Then digest and egest what you don't need = poo poo.

Cause what I find
Is a far cry from a fine line
Between the field of play
And the safety-craving, commentating sideline.
They aren't recommendations or F'ing guidelines!!!
It's not Syntax
It's A SIN TYPE!!
We've got lifetimes worth of Insights.
Yet do we squeeze the trigger when they're in sight?
Opportune times to use and shoot it on sight.
I've done so much work,
But I've done it
OFF
The
Job
Site

9-24-21

Same Sad

It’s
the
same
sad
in
Beijing
or
Baghdad.
Same
downcastness
on
my
friend
whose
father
got
lost
and
the
one
who
really
lost
his
dad.
I
noticed
this
in
my
raincoat.
Mist
frisked
me
amidst
the
gravestones.
It’s
that
identical
eyelid
slant
spanning
all
the
kids
and
chicks
at
Clemson
or
TriCounty.
That
exact
fever-
fueled
fear
on
the
Titanic
or
on
the
Bounty.
You
can
see
it
on
their
work-
worn
faces.
They
believe
they’re
going
places.
But
they’re
so
immobile
even
their
belief
is
in
stasis.
It’s
the
drawn
features
on
the
master
of
Tai
Lung
as
on
the
downtrodden
lover
whose
child’s
mother
has
died
young.
‘Tis
the
same
sad
that
spasms
grabbing
for
some
semblance
of
closure.
But
No,
sir.
You
are
not
permitted
to
lose
your
confidence
or
composure.
Now
these
cases
have
been
made,
but
have
you
ever
closed
Yours?

++

“You’re great with the people you care about, but if you don’t care about them, you could care less” – Josshua Findlay

9-29-21

Instead of encountering emotions and then believing I was forced to bear them within like a yoke on my heart, writing began as my mode of externalizing them. It is/ was this straining to get them out like forcing blood out of my skin all at once. Very not easy, and yet, there is so much relief in the release. There is no perfect art because it's that attempt to put all of oneself into something inanimate; life into something lifeless.

That's how I've recently been bestowed with the truth that we all have just as much capability as anyone else to write, draw, act, sing, dance, play, tell, or create art. (verb form of art?) I think that is where the beauty lies. That's not a wordplay at all. The beautifulness is in the disturbance of dormance, in the thrashing and agonizing of pulling your being outward into a form. It's tear-jerking.

9-19-21

I can feel the urgency
The
Pistols
Pistons
Building
Pressure
Everyone around me scurrying
MeanWhile, back at the ranch…
My grandma and parents
Cracking up at the idea
Of her joining the choir.

Life is down to the wire – Like in a Bentley hearse
Dead
Is the Twenty-First Century
But we're just making joyful noises
Singing Hallelujah with a new Silvestri
Congrats to the happy couple!
And at this ranch I
Found some courage.
I ran et past
Wizards and muggles
No , For real
She was housed out of the huddle.
With her bare feet,
Was care-free
And dared me
To come over there
Like to *Paree*
Perilously, I barely got past the
Grandparents, people who'd stand there and
Ne'er talk to me until they had their errands
B U T
Once only my fears remained,
I blew past their spells and starings.
You were super sweet
With your dimpled cheek
And strapless romper
I'm glad it didn't turn into Meet the Fockers!
But I just liked your style
And I really liked your smile
The ambiance that evening
Was just enough
to drive me
"Wild"

9/3/
/0/2
/1

TO THEM THE CLOSEST

How to even begin?

I thank you. You've been making me in whatever parts of my life you've been involved in. God has used you, and you might not have even been aware. It's incredible to me that many of the people have come and gone in the perfect proportions and durations. You have humbled me, struggled with me, joked, pranked, sang, probably bled, worked out with, argued, and mainly just grown with me.

We've had dramatic, thematic, and climactic conversations and occasions with each other for sure. Yet, they have guaranteed developed us into stronger, gentler, better listeners and lenders. Am I getting too wordy? <-(answer here)

Because Literally, it's much more strange to have this thing I made be read by you. I'm not one hundred percent sure why, but it's unlike anything I've done before. I'm not practicing katas or playing musical pieces or building something with materials that have a limited amount of variations to be used. I'm pulling my timeline and diving into my fallible knowledge and beating the ugly beasts up, and I'm bringing it all and heaving it into this somewhat coherent book. It's been hard. And fun. I've teared up at times. I've not been able to stop laughing. I've been pissed. I've been peaceful and grateful. I hope you can see you've been writing this just as much as I have.

I'm pretty positive that as you've read it or viewed the sketches and drawings you've thought something like, "He doesn't say that?" "Why did he draw that?" "When did he do that?" "Where did he learn that?" or my favorite, "He shouldn't have done that." At least, I hope you did. I probably don't have a satisfying response, lol, but it's been mine. My learning from you guys and heeding your advice and keeping my eyes on

Jesus as waves do what they do beneath my feet. It's been this immense mix of things that have brought me so far, and this little book has let me leave milestone markers along the way. I need it. I don't need you to understand it all. But I do need you.

I know that the people closest to me are gonna change. And I know that the people closest to me are gonna change. But I just thank you for letting me be part of your life. You may not write a book, (maybe one of you should though! Some competition hehe!) but you still have a story and a process and a progression. I love it. I love you.

There's this disgusting aspect of writing, and it's that you can only write one thing or idea or truth at a time. There's never a complete, entire, or whole thought or anything in life. It's like never seeing a whole tree or both sides of a hand at once. People are like that. Life is like that. BUT GOD (love those words together) will reveal and unveil and come near and I'll cry, and you'll cry, and we'll fall forwards and backwards at the same time and mmm. I just gotta stop. Why ruin it? We got this side today. It's gonna be legit.

ʒ ʒ

SUM UP
SUMMUM
SUMMATION

Σ Σ Σ Σ Σ Σ Σ Σ Σ Σ Σ Σ Σ Σ Σ Σ Σ Σ Σ Σ Σ Σ Σ Σ Σ Σ Σ Σ Σ Σ Σ Σ Σ Σ Σ Σ Σ

Now you've seen it: my attempt at being obedient. To this writing I'm an addict: like Captain Haddock. So in the future when I question if I should have alluded a pseudonym, please intercede for me in this way, "Lord, may they see YOU in him." It's been entirely mine. No if's, and's, or for's, nor but's about it. I'll always love it the most for God's hidden in my heart, and we found it. And I'm as equally thrilled for the fans as for my hater-base to be established. But when this reservist was actively purposed, I was also issued a sadness. For writing's my favorite

"pastime," but every slice of ink goes where the past is. This is as raw and unhindered as I'll ever be. If I'm granted the ingredients for a second "project," it'll be from a whole 'nother Timothy. Cause this one will do anything not to feel like an idiot. And I realize how idiotic that sentence is! But to tell my friends how I fail, fighting and writing to no avail, to leave myself at others' mercy makes my spirit's vessel frail and stale. Because so what if I don't seem bad to you? I'm the biggest loser when I look at Christ. If I live as if I don't despise myself, use people, get lonely, think the worst of things, mistreat so discretely, manipulate... etc. ... then I need to die! He knows that's what I want though. Set fire to my pyre, My Glory ablaze in a sacrificial suicide. I want to be done here. But He requires so much more from me = my Life. So I'm usually in one ditch or the other, hoping to just go out my way. Yet He pulls me out and poises me on His High Road = the highway. These ceaseless cycles make my head spin around, my thoughts always gyrate. I once saw it all from a level playing field, now I see it from the skyscape. I may act like my life's been hassle-free, but to quote Kevin McCallister, "I don't think so." But regardless, I'm a rapscallion, and no matter how badly of a rascal I'll be, my tongue will always confess, and I'll bow my knee. I've ingested the lessons. I'm detecting the blessings. I see the Author of this collection. He makes every second Convalescent. I love the growth, and I'm famished.
I can't wait to see the new world, it's outlandish.
Setting up this camp, like Miles Standish. I'm
not sure what's in store, but I know by
God I'll manage. I'll keep my eyes
open for the signs and the times,
and now I'm closed
until further
damage.

AFTERWORD

I have always looked at this as an album. Just like photo albums show us glimpses and snippets of lives, and just like music albums have separate songs to convey different meanings and feelings, this is my album. It's been a collection of five years' time where my life has been thrown all over the place. I've been a kid, and it's so chaotic being a kid these days. I've been morphing into an adult, and that's freaking hard these days too. I've been in love. I've been very out of love. I've laughed to degrees of personal injury. I've wept and wailed like a baby. I've been strong and fast. I've been brain dead and injured. I've hurt people and gotten hurt by people. I've changed so much and retained so much. And when I read any of this, I know it, and I love it, and I'm just so thankful for every piece of it. I know it's all God's, and I know that it would be an injustice to not craft this work and share this work with whomever I can, because it's not just my story. It's part of the story of how I have been saved by grace and changed through faith and how I have been given peace and purpose through pain. This has been my *Convalescence*; my healing process. And it never stops. We're all in the midst of life. We're all on upslopes and downsides, and we're in seasons with both blooming and disease. But hope hasn't shifted from its origin. No new developments have altered God's might and mercy. And this is just another cry from a flawed individual, but I know Him in whom I've put my trust. And He is worthy of it. So this is no longer mine. It has been, and it is His.

And It Is Well.

Salaam!
I found another one for ya.
How was it? Pretty cool? Pretty pernicious?
Do I seem touched by an angel or just slightly touched?
Any-which-either way, thank you for checking it out:)
Take it. Make it all your own.
It was given to me too.
Arrivederci.

ENDNOTES

1 Endorsements on pages 5-6 are real. Endorsements on pages 7-8 are fiction.

2 **Publisher's Note:** The interior design and layout was purposefully formatted to closely resemble the author's original journals. Similarly, we labored to make the cover design as true to the original design (which the author had in his mind's eye for years) as possible. As you've no doubt noticed, both the cover and interior designs break nearly every standard in professional publishing. But then, so does the author's decision to transparently present (in his own words) his "chaotic life as a kid…morphing into an adult…that's freaking hard." Nevertheless, from this chaos, we heard a melody that sings of Jesus the Christ, the author and finisher of our faith. The author who began this journal was different than the author who finished it. Christ never said our journey would be without difficulty or suffering, but He did say He would use all things to the good of those who love Him and who are called according to His purposes. Our prayer is that this transparent, rule-breaking, emotionally-charged journal will encourage young and old alike to surrender anew to the hands of our Master Potter.

3 Illustration was censored by the publisher.

4 Illustration was censored by the publisher.

Cowboy Up is a non-profit dedicated to suicide awareness and prevention through education and a message of hope. Learn more at **tncowboyup.com**.

SUICIDE PREVENTION LIFELINE

National Suicide Prevention Lifeline: Call 988.
The Lifeline provides 24/7, free and confidential support for people in distress. Learn more at **suicidepreventionlifeline.org**.

www.ingramcontent.com/pod-product-compliance
Lightning Source LLC
LaVergne TN
LVHW012328100826
845148LV00017B/539

9781613149065